Winds of War!

The ship pitched and swayed as choppy waves drove against it—then huge breakers slammed the hull as the winds tore at the sails.

"An Adept wind," Wulfston shouted. "We're under attack!"

Bracing his powers, Wulfston prepared himself for battle against an unseen enemy. But before he could act, a bolt of lightning struck the top of the main mast, exploding it into splinters. The ship was hopelessly crippled—they were trapped! Even as his mind insisted that there had to be a way to fight back, the deck exploded under Wulfston, tossing him high into the air before dropping him into the roiling madness of the storm-wild sea!

Wulfston's Odyssey

Jean Lorrah
and Winston A. Howlett

A SIGNET BOOK

NEW AMERICAN LIBRARY

SIGNET, SIGNET CLASSIC, MENTOR, ONYX, PLUME, MERIDIAN
and NAL BOOKS are published by NAL PENGUIN INC.,
1633 Broadway, New York, New York 10019

First Printing, November, 1987

1 2 3 4 5 6 7 8 9

PRINTED IN THE UNITED STATES OF AMERICA

Acknowledgments

The *Savage Empire* series is dedicated to the person who got me into professional sf writing and then encouraged me to start my own series:

Jacqueline Lichtenberg.

This book, of course, is also dedicated to Winston Howlett, who came up with the original idea, the African culture and the African characters, as well as collaborating on the book.

I would also like to thank the many readers who have sent comments about the first five books in the series; I hope you enjoy this sixth book in the *Savage Empire* universe. If you've missed the previous books, though, don't be afraid to start here. Each of the books can be read independently of the others.

If there are readers who would like to comment on this book, our publishers will forward letters to us. If you prefer, you may write to us at Box 625, Murray, KY 42071. If your letter requires an answer, be sure to enclose a stamped, self-addressed envelope.

All comments are welcome. I came to professional writing through fan writing and publishing, where there is close and constant communication between writers and readers. Thus I shall always be grateful for the existence of sf fandom, which has provided me with many exciting experiences, and through which I have met so many wonderful people—including the coauthor of this book!

Jean Lorrah

For my wife Gwen, who is my Tadisha.

Winston A. Howlett

Chapter One

Wulfston, Lord Adept of the Savage Empire, stared out at the strange ship approaching his coastline, several miles from the harbor. A merchant vessel by the look of her—so why did he see a one-vessel invasion fleet threatening his shores? A chill that owed nothing to the cool summer evening ran down his spine as the sunset's crimson painted the ship with shades of blood.

Gulls shrieked their disapproval at a boat being lowered from the anchored ship, the figures boarding it putting the vessel's size into perspective. Even from Wulfston's hilltop vantage point, it appeared huge and imposing.

The bay stallion Wulfston rode whinnied nervously and stamped the ground, snorting a challenge. The Lord Adept patted the beast's massive neck. "Easy, boy. We'll go down and see why these 'visitors' are sneaking ashore."

Urging Storm down the hillside, Wulfston caught from the corner of his eye the flashes of the watchers' message from a distant peak, reporting to his castle the arrival of the strange ship. He knew they would also report that the Lord of the Land was riding to investigate.

He let Storm choose the path and pace down to the beach. By the time they arrived, the boat was nearing shore. Wulfston counted eight people in it, two rowing, the others staring at him, whispering, pointing—

Cautiously, he braced his Adept powers, ready to call a greeting as soon as they were close enough to hear.

A fist of energy seized his heart!

7

Intense pain shot down his left arm. He realized, *They're Adepts!* and shoved away the assault with his own powers. *Or at least one of them is. But why are they attacking?*

Storm neighed and reared as fire bolts exploded around them. Wulfston leaped from the saddle into a fighting stance, deflecting the bolts sent to consume him. Ignoring pain, he concentrated on the people clambering from the boat. A wave of his hand and three of them collapsed, asleep on the sand.

Two others fanned out in opposite directions to divide his attention, splashing through the shallow surf. Wulfston dropped the one on the left and was turning toward the other when he realized they were diversions.

A lightning bolt shot from the sky, searing the air about him. He deflected most of its ferocity, but was enveloped in blinding light and Storm's screams.

His vision cleared while his nostrils flared at the smell of burning meat. Fighting nausea, he concentrated his anger on the tall man standing in the boat. With one urge of fury, he knocked his opponent out of the vessel, into an oncoming wave. A glance to the right dropped the other man unconscious.

Such steady use of his powers was weakening the Lord Adept, but he dared not stop until he had subdued them all. He charged the boat, staggering as the waves pounded at his knees, gambling that he was safe from those watching from the ship.

A veiled woman and a small boy huddled in the bottom of the boat, shaking with fear. Wulfston stared into the woman's eyes, forgetting everything—

He whirled at the sound of hoofbeats on the sand.

Lenardo and Julia pulled rein on their horses.

Lenardo's face reflected the grimness Wulfston felt. "Are you all right?" the Lord Reader asked.

Wulfston almost laughed at the question. If anyone could tell instantly whether someone was injured, it was Lenardo.

However, he replied, "Yes, I'm all right," surprised at the weariness in his tone. "But—"

Storm. The corpse was still smoldering. He shook his head at the senseless loss, and looked around at his captives. The man he had knocked into the water floated face down. He had to be pulled out before he drowned.

Lenardo swung from his horse and, with the ease of an active man in the prime of life, pushed past Wulfston's weakened efforts to drag the man ashore. Wulfston didn't have to ask if his attacker was alive; Lenardo would Read his condition and take appropriate action.

But Lenardo was demanding of Wulfston, "Why did you come out here to face these people alone?"

"I didn't," Wulfston replied tersely, insistently helping to drag the man ashore by his soggy cloak.

"Well, you must have had some reason to leave a celebration at your own castle and go riding this far south! I should have been Reading—"

"I was . . . restless," Wulfston replied slowly, analyzing his memories. "Something . . . drew me to this place, to these people."

"But why did they attack you?" Lenardo's daughter demanded.

"I don't know, Julia. I don't even know who they are."

"You don't?" the girl asked in a puzzled tone. "But Wulfston, they're all black—just like you!"

That fact had not escaped Wulfston's notice, but its significance had. The strange chill touched him again, stronger than before. Why would a shipload of people come, possibly all the way from Africa, to attack the only black Lord Adept in all the Savage Empire?

The answers had to wait until the next day. Some of Wulfston's guards and servants took the unexpected visitors back to his castle, fed them, healed those who had been injured, and put them all in guest rooms under heavy Adept guard.

Other guards rowed Wulfston and Lenardo to the merchant ship. Speaking in the tongue called Trader's Common, Wulfston ordered the Nubian captain and crew to move the ship up the coast into the harbor known as Dragon's Mouth. Having witnessed the Lord Adept's powers, they moved quickly to comply.

Interrogating the captain revealed little; the eight who had come ashore were the only passengers, and the tall man named Sukuru—the one Wulfston had knocked into the surf—had hired the ship for this journey, his intentions never stated.

A nod from Lenardo was all the assurance Wulfston needed that the captain was telling the truth.

The moon was high when the two lords finally returned to Castle Blackwolf. Word of the brief battle had already reached everyone there, so the cook had a lavish meal waiting for the Lord of the Land by the time he sat down in the banquet hall.

Though he had eaten dinner a few hours before, the heavy use of his powers made Wulfston feel like a starving man as he rapidly consumed enough food for three.

To eat his meal in peace, he had to fend off a dozen people who wanted to fuss over him.

He succeeded with all but his sister Aradia.

"But why did you go out there in the first place?" she demanded, sitting opposite him at the table.

He looked at her testily. "Aradia, why do you ask when you know I don't have the answer? Don't give me that innocent look. I know you and Lenardo were in contact with each other! For the last time, I don't know why I went riding along the cliffs, leaving a celebration I'm supposed to be hosting. Now, will you please leave me alone?"

Her look of puzzled hurt made him regret his harsh words. *What is wrong with me?* he asked himself.

"I'm sorry," he sighed, reaching across the table to

touch her hand. "I guess I'm more upset than I want to admit. Especially losing Storm like that."

She nodded in sympathy. Horses were still a rare and precious commodity in the Savage Empire, making the loss of such a fine stallion particularly acute.

She asked gently, "Do you think that it's possible that you might have . . . Read that that ship was there?"

He shook his head. "If I could sense a strange ship several miles away—which neither Lenardo nor Julia did until they started following me—then I should be able to pick up someone's thoughts nearby. But nothing has changed for me. I don't know what drew me into that confrontation, but it wasn't Reading. I'm still your mind-blind little brother," he said, forcing a chuckle.

Aradia returned his smile, then finally left him alone. As he watched her leave, Wulfston once again examined feelings he could not define.

For several months now, he had been plagued by dark moods and feelings of emptiness. His duties as a Lord Adept were no longer satisfying. He had decided he missed the camaraderie of the other ruling Adepts and Readers in the alliance. So when he had received the news that Aradia and Lenardo were expecting their first child, he had grasped the excuse to invite them for a celebration.

But the arrival of his friends and relatives had not eased his frustration. Indeed, he had begun to crave solitude before they had finished their first meal together! Hence the ride along the cliffs.

Was his feeling jealousy? After all, Aradia's Adept powers hadn't prevented her from learning to Read—the one goal in life he could not seem to achieve. Ironically, Wulfston had been the first of their group to theorize that Reading and Adept powers were the same, which Lenardo and Aradia later confirmed by gaining each other's talents. There was no reason in the world why Wulfston couldn't Read, but try as he would, he couldn't.

Another pressure was that he had neither wife nor heir.

His people were beginning to express concern as their lord approached the prime of life and the peak of his powers. If he was to produce an heir, now was the time to do it, while his powers were still growing. Lenardo would soon have two heirs, his adopted daughter Julia and his own child by Aradia. Wulfston wanted to feel joy at Lenardo's good fortune, but his words of congratulation rang hollow.

In a castle full of family and friends, with servants to respond to his slightest whim, the Lord of the Land felt totally alone.

The next day, under guard of minor Adepts, the "visitors" from the ship were brought before Wulfston in his audience chamber.

Wulfston rarely sat on his throne, but his father Nerius had carefully taught both his son and his daughter the techniques of rule. Pomp and ceremony seemed to come more naturally to Aradia, but Wulfston felt the appropriateness of his position this day.

For several long moments he said nothing to those who had attacked him, letting them stare at the Lord of the Land and the people flanking him: Lenardo and Aradia seated in places of honor to his right, Julia and Rolf, Wulfston's Reader, to his left. Readers and Adepts all, a formidable assembly.

Sukuru was the group's leader, though he lacked the bearing of a Lord Adept. Authority did not sit well upon his gaunt frame, and his ebony skin seemed to blanch under Wulfston's gaze.

It was apparent that Sukuru was badly shaken by his encounter. At first Wulfston assumed it was because he had been so easily defeated. It turned out, however, that the newcomers had not expected to find the Lord of the Land on the cliffs, wrapped in a plain woolen cloak. Rather, when they saw another black man they feared he had been sent by their enemies to thwart their expedition.

"For it is well known even unto our lands," Sukuru explained, speaking Trader's Common with a heavy accent, "that the most excellent Lord of the Black Wolf is a great and noble ruler. We thought to find you as you are now, most gracious lord, crowned in gold and seated upon a throne. Because of our enemies, we approached by stealth, rather than have our ship enter your harbor. Please forgive us for your injuries, and the death of your beautiful steed—"

"You are forgiven," Wulfston said impatiently. "Tell me why you've come here."

"Most excellent lord," Sukuru explained, "we have traveled over vast distances to implore your help. The lands of Africa are held in the grip of a powerful witch queen named Z'Nelia. From her throne in Johara she spins her webs of power, ensnaring all who live there. Those who dare speak out or rebel against her harsh rule or insane proclamations are condemned to death—or to slavery.

"We who have come seeking your help represent many tribes and peoples who share a dream of freedom—freedom from Z'Nelia's tyranny. But we lack the power to depose her. Besides her own formidable powers, she has many followers with powers of their own, as well as a huge and powerful army."

"But why would you come so far to seek *my* help?" Wulfston asked.

"Word of your exploits has reached our lands," the emissary replied. "There is a song which tells of your battle against the armies of the Black Dragon, how you defeated him in single combat."

Wulfston heard Julia smother a snicker, and knew his other friends found this exaggeration equally amusing. Indeed, he had difficulty restraining his own laughter—and realized that it felt good, the first spontaneous laughter he had enjoyed in some time.

"That song," he explained when he could reply with dignity to match the man's sincerity, "was created by a bard seeking favor in my court. East of here, in the city of Zendi, you would hear a much different version, celebrating the exploits of my sister and her husband." He gestured toward Aradia and Lenardo, enjoying the puzzled look that crossed Sukuru's face when Wulfston identified the pale blond Aradia as his sister. "In truth, it took our combined powers and those of many others to defeat Drakonius."

"Nevertheless," Sukuru pressed on, "you are the most powerful ruler in these lands. Is that not so?"

"No," Wulfston replied patiently, "that is not so. Our alliance is so powerful because it is precisely that: an alliance. Lenardo, Aradia, Lilith, Torio, Melissa—there are many of us."

"Then you are . . . merely a vassal to some higher lord?" Sukuru asked.

"No," Wulfston said firmly. "We are allies. And if your Z'Nelia is so powerful, the only way to defeat her is to join your powers with those of others who oppose her. Surely, if she is as evil as you claim, you will easily find others to support you. Why come to our lands seeking a champion?"

"You do not understand our situation, lord," Sukuru replied. "Let Chulaika explain."

He gestured to the young woman Wulfston had found in the boat. She came forward hesitantly, her little boy clinging to his mother's skirts. Chulaika was wrapped in veils, only her eyes visible, her lower face obscured by a soft dark cloth that rippled with her breath.

"Most powerful Lord," she murmured, her voice trembling, "our people are oppressed, our men taken into slavery, our children threatened. Many of our young people that have shown strong powers have been killed— murdered by Z'Nelia because they might oppose her rule. Please, Lord Wulfston, come to our aid. Only a great lord like yourself can help us."

There was something compelling about Chulaika's eyes. Wulfston was able to break his gaze from hers only when

Sukuru said, "You are a Son of Africa, Lord. Surely you will not refuse to help your own people?"

"My own people," said Wulfston, "are right here. I was not born in your land, but in the Aventine Empire, where my parents were proud to have earned citizenship." He did not add that they had been killed by their fellow citizens when their son exhibited forbidden powers.

"My people," he continued, "are still recovering from the suffering Drakonius caused them, still learning to trust our alliance, still building a new life upon the ruins of the old. I will consult with my allies to determine what help we can offer. But you must understand that I cannot leave my lands unattended to go adventuring in yours." Yet he had to admit, once he had so abruptly dismissed the petitioners, that perhaps his shortness was caused by temptation.

It was the conflict with Drakonius that had first brought Wulfston out of Aradia's shadow. Furthermore, in the days of conflict decisions had been easy: they fought Drakonius, they fought the would-be usurpers who had tried to attack their alliance after his defeat, and they fought the invading Aventines. The right thing to do had been so clear then.

Nowadays it seemed he dealt only with arguments over boundaries, or charges and countercharges in business disputes. And the ever-present question of his heir.

Wulfston decided to talk to Lenardo, who had become as close as a brother in the days when they had learned to work together against their common enemies. Somehow the Master Reader, who was hardly five years older than Wulfston, seemed to have the wisdom of the ages.

"Are you going to tell me what's bothering you?" Lenardo asked when they were alone. "You're so braced for defense that I can't even Read your feelings."

"I couldn't get the truth out of those people," Wulfston replied, going to the other problem on his mind. "Under all that bowing and scraping—"

"They were appealing to your ego," said Lenardo. "When that didn't work, Sukuru attacked your pride."

"Oh, I got the insult, all right. Sukuru is not the clever diplomat he thinks he is."

"Agreed." Lenardo looked at him expectantly.

Finally Wulfston said, "Did you—? I know your Reader's Code prevented you from probing them deeply, but surely you got some surface impressions?"

Lenardo frowned, staring at his hands. On his left glittered the ring which symbolized his marriage to Aradia, their two emblems, wolf and dragon, intertwined.

Wulfston had had the matching rings made by the finest goldsmith in his lands, as his wedding gift to his sister and her husband. While it symbolized specifically the marriage of these two, it was also emblematic of their entire alliance: neither beast could be separated from the other without breaking the ring, just as no member of their alliance dared fail the rest without endangering the existence of the Savage Empire.

Finally Lenardo said, "I think you got the same impression I did, Wulfston: our uninvited guests were telling the truth. As far as it went."

"Meaning I didn't ask the right question."

"Meaning they didn't answer it. They were very open and forthright about what they wanted you to do, but highly evasive the moment you asked why." The Reader frowned, rubbing his neatly bearded chin as if deciding whether to confide what he had learned in a way Readers considered unscrupulous. Then he fixed dark eyes on Wulfston and said, "I wonder how much they really know? The description of Z'Nelia, for example, sounds so much like Portia—"

"To you, perhaps," said Wulfston. "Besides, Portia was a Reader."

"Which is why she could not act openly, as this African Adept can. But you are right, Wulfston. What made me think of Portia was the image of the spider with her webs spun throughout the kingdom. That was how Portia seemed to me, once I discovered her evil. I'm sure this Z'Nelia is quite different, probably more like Drakonius."

"So you think we should help Sukuru and Chulaika?"

"Not until we find out what they're hiding. The impression I got was that they are trying to use you. Their talk of freedom for their people is a sham. What they really want is the throne of Nubia—perhaps all of Africa—for themselves."

"That ragtag band?" Wulfston snorted. "Who would sit on the throne? Sukuru? He's only a minor Adept."

"Yes," agreed Lenardo, "they're all either weak Adepts or low-level, untrained Readers. Their combined talents were nothing against you, and you're not yet at the height of your powers. If their Z'Nelia is mature and as powerful as Drakonius was, no wonder they're looking for help."

"Perhaps they came here," Wulfston suggested, "because they knew I wouldn't be interested in claiming a throne on another continent, and so would leave it to them?"

"Unlikely. They seemed honestly amazed that we have an alliance of equals. It sounds to me as if their Adepts are still fighting one another, with the strongest subjecting all the others. So with his limited powers, I cannot see how Sukuru thinks to hold Z'Nelia's throne, even if you should gain it for him."

Wulfston nodded. "Well, Read whatever you can at dinner without breaking your Oath. Even if I can't Read, I know there's something more than our guests have told us so far!"

Hoping to draw Sukuru and Chulaika out, Wulfston provided plenty of wine, and he and Lenardo, Julia, and Aradia told the story of the defeat of Drakonius—rather than letting the bard sing his distorted version.

Zanos and Astra, another Adept/Reader married couple, joined the group at the long table. Wulfston was rather surprised that they had nothing to say, for Z'Nelia sounded much like the sorcerers they had encountered in Madura, Zanos' native land, from where they had recently returned. Perhaps they were biding their time, unwilling to reveal what they knew.

There were too many unrevealed secrets about that journey—especially why Torio, the blind Reader, had not returned from it. When the young man had developed the gift of prophecy, and known thereby that the woman he loved must seek her fortune in the frozen north, he had followed her there . . . and apparently lost her to Maldek, a Master Sorcerer. But then, instead of returning with Zanos and Astra, Torio had gone off on his own—to the east, Zanos had said, following some whim of his own.

And leaving Wulfston without a Reader. He had Rolf, of course, and several Magister Readers as well as numerous Dark Moon Readers who had come to work in his lands. But Torio had been friend and equal as none of these could be. Blast Torio's prophecies anyway! What had they done but lose him Melissa and send him off to seek his fortune away from all his friends? Didn't Torio realize his absence weakened their alliance?

But there was no use wishing for Torio. For the moment, Wulfston had Lenardo, the finest Reader ever known, to help him in this delicate situation. And Lenardo was explaining to Wulfston's guests their entangled relationships.

"So Julia is my adopted daughter, though I don't think either of us often remembers that she's adopted. Aradia is my wife, and that makes her brother Wulfston my brother, too."

Sukuru asked, "How comes it, Lord Wulfston, that these pale folk claim you kin?"

"Ties of love may be as strong as ties of blood," he replied. "When I was only three years old, I showed the first evidence of my powers."

A swift glance passed from Sukuru to Chulaika. The woman had worn her veils even to the table, slipping bits of food up beneath her silken mask; so that when she caught Wulfston looking at her she dropped her eyes and he could tell nothing more of her expression.

Wulfston continued, "Aradia's father, Nerius, stole me from the Aventine Empire, for the village folk would have murdered me for showing Adept powers in a land where only Reading was acceptable. They did kill my parents and my sister. Nerius was unable to rescue them, but he adopted me, and that is how he became my father and Aradia my sister."

"We grew up together," Aradia put in. "It was no different than if we had had the same parents by blood; we were playmates, we got into mischief together, and we fought and made up, just the way any other brother and sister would. Because our Adept powers set us apart from other children, we were actually closer than most brothers and sisters. I had been a very lonely child before Father brought Wulfston home."

"And I was very young," Wulfston added. "No, I never forgot my birth parents. Nerius had known them for a long time, and so now I can't tell you which are my own memories and which are stories Father told me. He wanted me to remember my heritage, how proud my parents were that they had earned their way out of slavery and become Aventine citizens." *And then I developed the wrong power.*

Aradia stepped into the pause. "So you see, our alliance is like a family—we love and trust one another, even when we are under attack. And now that we are safe and secure, with our friends to protect us from unforeseen dangers, Lenardo and I are having our own child. She will not be only our daughter; she will be Julia's sister, and Wulfston's niece. That is the kind of family alliance you must have to fight a tyrant."

Sukuru nodded. "Yes, we understand, although I must confess I am amazed. Perhaps, then, most gracious Lord, you will advise us in our quest? Explain to us how power-

ful rulers may be made to work together instead of battling one another?"

"Not all can," replied Wulfston. "Some of our supposed
allies proved false. They were with us when they thought
we had a chance of winning, but turned to Drakonius
when he seemed to have the advantage. But if you can
find leaders who understand that striving for the good of
their people is what keeps them strong, those are the
lords who will aid you in your cause to rid your land of a
tyrant."

Sukuru rose, and bowed to Wulfston. "We will heed
your advice, most excellent Lord. Now"—he gestured to
one of his retainers, who had stood guard near the door to
the great hall all through the meal—"let us present you
with a wine of our country—a toast to our success in
gaining from you the means to save our land!"

The man handed Sukuru an ornate vessel, slim and
beautifully shaped, with two handles near the narrow mouth.
This wine bottle could not sit on the table, for the bottom
was pointed rather than flat. It appeared to be of fired
clay, but it was painted in brilliant colors that flashed like
jewels.

Once the wax seal had been broken all the wine had to
be poured out. Everyone at the table received a generous
portion. Sukuru raised his goblet. "To the defeat of Z'Nelia—
and anything we must do to free our land from her evil!"

The wine was sweet, and heavily spiced; they would
need no sweet to end their meal.

Suddenly Aradia, who was seated between Wulfston
and Lenardo, leaned over and whispered in her brother's
ear, "Come to our room after dinner. Lenardo has Read
something."

Wulfston leaned forward to look at his sister's husband,
but Lenardo was taking a drink of wine. Obviously he did
not want their guests to know what he had discovered.

Wulfston took another swallow of wine and realized that
the sweet spiciness was creating thirst more than quench-

ing it. And he should drink no more wine; he'd had enough during all the toasts.

He deliberately set his cup aside, and signaled to his butler. "Get a dryer wine from the cellars," he instructed, "and some fruit juice for me."

"And for me," Aradia put in. "I should not drink more wine tonight, either."

Eager to know what Lenardo had found out—and frustrated at the knowledge that the Readers at his table already knew it—Wulfston wished he could cut the dinner short. But protocol demanded that sweets and fruits be offered, and then entertainment provided.

His impatience grew as his musicians performed, and he found himself yawning. He was bored with the music. Well, what was the good of being Lord of the Land if he couldn't stop the entertainment when he grew tired of it?

At the end of a piece he rose. "Thank you for your fine music, my friends. Jareth, take them off and reward them suitably. Now, though, I know our guests are tired. My servants are available for anything you might need."

They dispersed to their own rooms. Wulfston took off his crown and chains of office, as well as the heavily embroidered tabard he had worn for the state dinner. Wrapped in a light woolen robe against the castle's chill, he felt much more comfortable. In fact almost too comfortable. . . .

He was cold—cold and clammy. His head ached, and when he moved it hurt even more. Forcing his eyes open a slit, Wulfston groaned at the stab of pain from sunlight piercing his brain.

He lay still, calling up healing heat, and almost fell asleep again as it did its work. Finally, though, the poisons in his blood were purged, and he rose to his feet.

Although the sun was high in the sky, the castle was silent.

In the hallway the guard slumped against the wall, so

deep in sleep that Wulfston had to touch him to be sure
he wasn't dead. The man woke at his touch, though; he
had been put to sleep with Adept powers, not drugged.

"Go—wake the other guards and secure the castle!"
Wulfston instructed, and hurried down the stairs. *We are
wide open for attack!*

In the great hall the board still sat with the crumb-laden
cloth upon it. Most of the dishes had been cleared away,
but the wine goblets stood at their place. Those where
Sukuru and his people had sat were still full.

Whatever Lenardo had Read when Sukuru had handed
out the wine had been a ruse—something to attract the
attention of all the Readers, so that no one would think to
Read the wine.

In the kitchen, Wulfston found the fire out, and Jareth
sprawled on the floor. There was no sign of the musicians.

He touched his retainer, and the older man moaned
softly as he tried to wake up. *He probably drank more of
the spiced wine than I did.* Wulfston thought, and sent
healing fire to cleanse the man's blood. Jareth slumped
back to sleep.

As Wulfston turned away, his cook came running into
the kitchen in her nightgown. "Oh, me lord! What's happened? No one woke this morning—not one of the servants
is up!"

"It's not your fault," he assured her. "Sukuru put everyone into Adept sleep. Make a big pot of strong tea, and
start breakfast. Jareth should waken soon. Send him to
wake up everyone at the dairy and the stables."

Wulfston, meanwhile, dashed back up the stairs. As he
expected, he found Sukuru's room empty. Foreboding in
his heart, he knocked at the door to Lenardo and Aradia's
room. When there was no response, he opened the door,
passed their servants sleeping soundly in the anteroom,
and went into the inner chamber.

Aradia lay alone in the bed, her pale hair spread neatly
across the pillow as if she had not moved all night long.

Wulfston touched her brow, letting healing power flow before he placed a fingertip gently between her eyes.

His sister blinked up at him. "Wulfston what—? Why have I slept so late?" She sat up, looking around. "Where's Lenardo?"

"Aradia, we were drugged," Wulfston explained. "The wine Sukuru served us—"

"Drugged?!" Aradia's naturally pale skin grew bone-white, and she clutched her arms across her abdomen. "The baby! Oh, Wulfston—get Lenardo to Read whether our baby's been harmed!"

"I don't know where he's gone," Wulfston replied.

"Aradia? Wulfston?" It was Julia's voice at the door to the adjoining chamber.

"Julia, come in!" Aradia cried. "Can you Read where Lenardo is?"

"Not in the castle," the girl replied at once. "What's the matter?"

"Please," Aradia told her, "Read the baby—see if she's been poisoned."

"Poisoned!" Julia's eyes grew round with horror, but she laid a hand on Aradia's only slightly swelling abdomen and concentrated. "No," she said at last. "I can't Read anything but a healthy baby, Aradia, and I'm sure Father will confirm that."

"You don't have a headache, Aradia," Wulfston realized. "Your body instinctively protected your child. You probably went directly into healing sleep and purged the poison from your blood at once. The drug knocked me out so completely that I couldn't cleanse it away until I woke this morning."

"I took only a small taste of the wine," said Aradia. "But where is Lenardo?" she demanded. "Wulfston—?"

"Our uninvited guests have gone," he replied. "Perhaps he followed them." But he braced himself so that neither woman could Read him, knowing that if the drug had kept someone with Wulfston's Adept powers unconscious all night, Lenardo would not have been the one to waken first.

Julia had taken on the abstract look of a Reader seeking something far away. "I can Read as far as the harbor," she said, "and I can't find Father anywhere." Then she gasped, and her eyes focused on Wulfston's face. "The ship! Wulfston, the ship is gone!"

Julia's powers, while impressive for so young a Reader, could not extend far out to sea. So Wulfston went to waken Zanos and Astra, for Astra was a Magister Reader who would be taking the tests for the Master level some-day soon. If necessary, she could leave her body to Read for the ship, a skill Julia was not quite old enough to begin learning.

By this time, Zanos and Astra had been wakened by their servants and had cleansed the effects of the drug from their own bodies. When Wulfston told them what had happened, Astra said, "You think they kidnapped Lenardo? Why would they do that?"

"They drugged us," said Zanos. "I wouldn't put any-thing past people who would do that—and then steal a man away from his family." He picked up the sword which lay ready beside his bed, ready to set out to Lenardo's rescue.

"First find out if he's on that ship," said Wulfston.

"Of course." Astra concentrated, her husband standing guard while her attention was elsewhere. While Astra was typically Aventine, tall and slender, with dark hair and eyes, Zanos was Maduran—a huge, red-haired man a head taller than Wulfston, with the well-developed body of a gladiator.

That had been his profession, but he was far from the stereotype of the stupid warrior. Still, Zanos was an uncom-plicated man, strong in his loyalties, devoted to his wife, and determined when he set his mind to something.

Zanos and Astra were here as representatives of Lilith, a

Lady Adept whose lands lay several days' ride to the north. Hers were the border lands, where there was still the danger of attack from those who sought to test the vulnerability of the unwieldy amalgam of former Aventine Empire and savage lands.

Had it not been for Zanos and Astra, Lilith would have lost her castle to marauders three years ago, when she and her son were away helping their allies to the south. Thus Lilith was determined to stay home now, because she had promised Aradia that later, when she came close to her time, Lilith would come to see her through the birth of her first child.

Wulfston watched Zanos and Astra, wishing again that he could Read—if only just as well as Zanos or Aradia, for even the smallest ability allowed one to "listen in," as it were, to a stronger Reader. Thus Zanos would be Reading through Astra now, as he stood by her protectively. He would know at once what she found out about Lenardo, while Wulfston had to wait impatiently for them to tell him.

Finally Astra cried, "I've found the ship. Lenardo is on board. He is locked in the hold, but he's still asleep. I couldn't waken him. Sukuru has added Adept sleep to the effects of the drug."

"Mawort damn them to the torture pit!" said Zanos. "Lord Wulfston, I'm ready to help you rescue Lord Lenardo. Astra?"

"Of course," she replied. "How soon can you get a ship ready, my lord? With the Adept power we can command we'll soon overtake them. The important thing is not to let them get out of Reading range, since we don't know where in Africa they're going."

"Just let me get my hands on that Sukuru," muttered Zanos, and Wulfston recognized that he was controlling fury. For a moment he didn't understand Zanos' concern over a man who was only an acquaintance, but then he remembered that the gladiator had been stolen from his own homeland as a child and, like Wulfston's own parents, sold into slavery in the Aventine Empire. There he had been trained to fight in the arena, forced to earn again the freedom he had been born to.

"I'll call for a ship," said Wulfston, and hurried downstairs. Jareth was now awake and alert, and he set the man to making arrangements while he went to tell Aradia—

"Most excellent lord."

Wulfston whirled at the soft voice speaking from a shadowed alcove.

The veiled woman, Chulaika, stood with her child huddled against her.

"You! What is the meaning of this?" Wulfston demanded.

"I have stayed to guide you, most excellent Lord," she replied firmly, although he could see the fear behind the determination in her eyes. "You will need my help during your long journey to Africa."

"So!" he breathed. "Sukuru kidnapped Lenardo in order to force me into your conflict with Z'Nelia. Well, you've underestimated us, woman! Lenardo's not our only good Reader. We've already found the ship, and we'll catch up with it by sundown."

"Begging your pardon, Lord Wulfston, but you will not. You will need my guidance to find Sukuru—and to rescue your sister's husband."

"Never mind," he said impatiently. "Go pack your things. You're going with us, so I can hand you back to Sukuru. And frankly, I don't care what he does with you!"

As he turned away from her, Chulaika said, "Pack for a journey, Lord Wulfston. If you do not, you will find yourself in a far country with naught but the clothes on your back."

Wulfston quickly dressed for travel, but he wasn't fast enough to avoid Aradia. She came into his room as he was turning his small private coffer out onto the bed. There

were enough gold and silver coins to buy anything he
might need, should Chulaika's warning prove true.

Aradia wore a serviceable light woolen gown in her
favorite violet, which matched her eyes. Her hair was
braided and bound simply about her head, and she carried
a hooded cloak. "Hurry, Wulfston," she said, sounding
just the way she had when they were children. "We don't
want to miss the tide!"

"Aradia—"

"I'm going with you."

"No, you're not," he told her firmly.

"Wulfston, it's my husband they've taken!"

"And that's his child you're carrying," he countered.
"You were fortunate that the drug did not harm the baby—
for Sukuru still let you drink it after he knew you were
pregnant. You don't know what these people are capable
of if they have no care for the health of an unborn babe.
Will you be as careless as they are? Will you take your
child into the midst of Adept conflict?"

"I can take care of my baby and myself," Aradia insisted.
Not wanting to argue, Wulfston turned away from her
angry glare and began putting the coins into a leather
pouch.

Suddenly his muscles went stiff, as Aradia sought to
prove her strength by controlling him. He should have
expected it, it was something she had often done to win an
argument when they were children. Her powers had always been superior, as she was five years older than he.

But this time it took only a moment's concentration for
Wulfston to shake off Aradia's Adept hold.

He turned swiftly, showing her plainly that her strength
was waning with her pregnancy. "You see? Aradia, you
just don't have your full powers right now."

But as he saw tears spring to her eyes he moved quickly
to comfort her. "Please . . . we both know it's best that
you stay here. I know it won't help for me to tell you not

to worry, but I promise you this: I will bring Lenardo back to you, safe and sound. I swear it!"

Captain Laren, owner of the *Night Queen*, had more than a few objections to his ship's being pressed into service as a pursuit vessel. But he needed continued use of Dragon's Mouth for his merchant business, so a deal was quickly struck.

Wulfston boarded ship with Zanos, Astra, and a number of his own people. Even old Huber, a grizzled warrior who was a water talent, volunteered for the mission. Wulfston put Chulaika and her son in the boat in which he was rowed out to the *Night Queen*—just in time to sail with the tide.

"You see?" he told her. "My people always work together. We'll easily catch up to Sukuru, and trade you for Lenardo."

"You will see," was all the woman would say from under her veil.

Since Wulfston was the only one on board with weather-changing talents, the other Adepts supported him as he created a strong wind that quickly carried the ship out to sea.

But as the shoreline vanished, Zanos said, "We can't keep this up much longer, Lord Wulfston. We'll be exhausted by the time we catch up with Sukuru's ship."

"You're right," Wulfston conceded, letting the wind die down. "We must conserve our strength. This is going to take longer than I thought, and Sukuru isn't going to give up Lenardo without some . . . 'persuasion.'"

"Perhaps we can use natural weather conditions," Astra suggested. "I can Read a minor squall building south of here. If we could guide its winds this way, it would take much less work to catch Sukuru."

Wulfston nodded. "A good suggestion, Astra. Let's try it."

By the time the brisk stormwinds filled the *Night Queen's*

ils, the sun was on the western horizon. Some minutes later, a tiny black dot could be seen in the center of the crimson sphere.

"She's still several hours ahead of us, Lord Wulfston!" the captain called out over the cheering. "We won't catch 'er till after midnight!"

"But we *will* catch them," Wulfston replied, glancing at Chulaika. She avoided his eyes as she lifted her son into her arms.

CRACK! A bolt of lightning struck the mainmast, sending down a shower of splinters.

"It's Sukuru!" Zanos bellowed. "He's turning the storm against us!"

A second bolt struck the bow before Wulfston could move to deflect it. Flames sprang up in the foredeck, but the Lord Adept extinguished them with a moment's concentration.

"Combine your powers to shield the ship!" he commanded the Adepts. If he could put everyone on Sukuru's ship to sleep—

Another loud *CRACK!* came from the mainmast, this time from within. The captain barked out orders.

Astra cried out, "The mast! It's going to—"

It split diagonally, the upper half becoming a spear hurtling down at Wulfston's people. Trying to work with gravity, he put his powers to angling the missile away from the people aboard.

Zanos and two of the other Adepts added their strength to his, but it was not enough to send the debris over the side. The jagged point ripped through the starboard side of the deck and came out the hull, just below the waterline.

Captain Laren shouted, "Hard to port! We'll have to make it to one of the Turtle Islands and beach 'er, or we'll sink for sure!"

Wulfston started to object, but knew the captain was right. The Adepts could do little more than keep the ship afloat for a league or so, until they reached shallow waters. And then at least a day would be spent making repairs.

Very clever, Sukuru, But you won't escape me!

While Huber and the others helped the crewmen make temporary repairs, Wulfston strode angrily to Chulaika, who was still holding her son, still avoiding his eyes . . . but somehow seemed less fearful of the Lord Adept than she had been before.

"Very well, woman. Tell me were Sukuru is taking Lenardo."

"Show me your charts," she replied, "and I will plot your course." At least she had the dignity not to say "I told you so."

Later, Wulfston stood watching the sun set. Astra and Zanos joined him. "Don't worry," said Zanos, "we'll catch up and rescue Lenardo."

Wulfston nodded. "Yes, but we may have to go all the way to Africa to do it. I've been trying all day not to think about the prophecy Torio made before he left with you for Madura. He told me, 'Your fate is linked with Lenardo's, but it is your own destiny you will seek far away, only to find where you began.' So here I am, sailing far away because of Lenardo. I wonder—what does the rest of the prophecy mean? Does 'where I first began' mean Nubia, the land of my ancestors? I don't know anything about it! I may look like Sukuru and the other black people, but they are not *my* people. If my destiny truly lies among them, will I ever see home again?"

Chapter Two

*T*he repairs on the *Night Queen* took nearly two days. By the time the ship put to sea again, Sukuru's vessel was beyond Astra's Reading range, even out of body. Wulfston was forced to depend entirely on the course Chulaika plotted.

He was not sure he could trust her, even in that regard. Apparently she was following Sukuru's plan to force the Lord Adept to travel to Africa, but what if all this were part of an even larger scheme—a plot against the Savage Empire?

Wulfston remembered leaving Aradia and Jareth on the dock in his homeland. "What if this is a ruse to divide our strength?" he had wondered aloud. "Enemies have tried to split our alliance before. Sukuru might have friends— strong Adepts and Readers—who hope that all of us will sail off to rescue Lenardo, leaving our lands unprotected.

"You may be right, my lord," Jareth had agreed. "We must expect the unexpected."

"Indeed," Wulfston nodded. "If I'd done that last night, we wouldn't have lost Lenardo, would we?"

"Don't blame yourself, my brother," Aradia said softly. "We were all fooled. Not even Lenardo Read Sukuru's intent."

Wulfston did not forgive himself so easily. Somewhere deep inside him, a voice whispered, "You should have known. You saw the signs and ignored them."

What signs? he asked himself. *What should I have known, but didn't?*

The vast ocean yielded no answers, merely beckoned to his mind, drawing him beyond the railing, seducing him into forgetting all his concerns and losing himself in—

"Lord Wulfston?"

He spun around, bracing his powers—to find Astra beside him, startled by his reaction.

"I'm sorry," he said, smiling to cover his embarrassment. "I didn't hear you. I guess I was experiencing that thing sailors are always talking about: 'the spell of the sea.'"

"Is this your first time sailing to a foreign land?" the Reader asked.

"My first time out to sea," he confessed. "My first experience of being totally surrounded by deep water. It's beautiful, but I'm beginning to understand how it must have seemed to your fellow Aventine Readers when the invasion fleet left their empire—how vulnerable they must have felt when I sent the storm to drive away their ships from my lands."

"You're thinking about the Readers who drowned?"

"Yes, and how easily the same thing could happen to us," he said grimly. "Sukuru has two days' head start. If we can't close the gap, we may find someone waiting on the African coast to drive *us* away!"

"Z'Nelia?"

"Or one of her allies. From what Captain Laren tells me, the city of Johara is near Africa's east coast. This course that Chulaika has plotted is taking us to the west, a thousand miles from Johara. Even if this witch-queen is as powerful as Sukuru said, her powers can't possibly reach that far. But if she has Adept friends on the west coast . . ."

"Wouldn't it be more likely that Sukuru and *his* allies would be there? If he's trying to force you to help you depose a powerful sorceress, surely he's not going to lead you into a trap!"

"How can we be sure of anything? Your husband agrees these people can't be trusted." She followed his glance down the length of the deck to where Chulaika sat at the stern, sharing a meal with her son. "For instance, what are your impressions of her?"

"Hard to say. She seems to have as much Adept talent as I do, which is not much. She doesn't seem to want to be here, away from her homeland, any more than we want to be away from ours. But she's determined not to show it. And you must have noticed how protective she is of her son, Chaiku. Aren't you curious as to why a four-year-old never speaks, only cries and makes grunting sounds?"

"With all that's been going on, I hadn't noticed," Wulfston admitted. "Have you Read his physical condition?"

"This morning, before we left the island. It didn't tell me much. His throat and voice box seem to be normal, which should mean that the disorder is in his brain. When I asked Chulaika if he had ever had the power of speech, she became defensive, bracing her powers. So I left her alone."

" 'Our children threatened,' " Wulfston said, quoting what Chulaika had told them in his throne room. "Perhaps he is a victim of more than just a threat."

Just then Captain Laren strode over to them, looking very serious. "Lord Wulfston, I'm sorry. From my calculations, even with all you Adepts helping, this ship cannot possibly catch up with that African merchantman. They'll reach the African coast at least a day before we will."

Wulfston stared at the man, not knowing where to vent his frustration. He expelled it in a controlled breath, then said, "Just get us there as quickly as you can."

"And then?" Laren asked.

"I don't know," the Lord Adept said quietly, then walked to the stern of the ship. Chulaika looked up as he approached her. "You win, it seems. In a few days I will be in your land."

"But not helping us fight against Z'Nelia," she said

softly, "so it is no victory at all. I told my master that his plan would not work."

"You're Sukuru's *slave*?" he asked. He had assumed that the two were allies.

" 'Servant' would be the best word in this language. He saved me and my son from being sold into slavery, but . . . sometimes obeying his wishes seems no better than serving a slavemaster. If only you knew how much your help is needed in Africa—"

"We've already been through that," he said firmly. "I haven't changed my mind. When we reach Africa, I will do whatever I have to do to rescue Lenardo, but I will not become a part of your rebellion!"

"Then what do you require of me, Lord Wulfston?"

Rather than make further demands, Wulfston decided to try another tack. "I'll make a bargain with you, Chulaika," he said softly. "I must know more about what I will face in your homeland. If you will teach me your native language, and as much as possible about your lands and customs, I will do what I can to cure your son's muteness. With the help of Magister Astra's Reading powers—"

Chulaika's reaction was a strange, bitter laugh as she drew the child close. "You cannot help him, Lord Wulfston. No Healer can. The silence of his tongue is the mark of Shangonu, our god. It is His will that Chaiku not speak—to oppose the will of the god would bring disaster upon us."

Wulfston was amazed at her response. "You believe that it's wrong for him to be healed?"

"Shangonu forbids it. You cannot understand," she insisted firmly. "You are not of my people, know nothing of our ways." Although her voice remained soft, its intensity increased. "I will teach you what I can, most excellent lord, but there are some things about my homeland that even you, a Son of Africa, will never be able to learn."

Zanos and Astra were included in the language lessons. With the powers of concentration studied by both Readers and Adepts, their progress was swift, and soon all three were capable of intelligible, if not colloquial, conversation in the language of Chulaika's people, the Zionae.

In the process they learned that Africans perceived Reader and Adept powers much differently than the Aventines or savages did. Readers in Africa were called Seers, while Adepts were generally called Movers. Minor Adepts were known by their principal talent: healers, firemakers, rainbringers, and so forth.

Readers were often inducted into religious orders, to use their powers for social good. The fate of a person with both Reading and Adept powers depended on where he lived; in some areas such a person might become part of a coven of wizards while in other tribes a Reader/Adept would be a natural ruler.

During one lesson, Astra told Chulaika, "Only in the past few years have our Readers and Adepts begun to learn each other's powers. Are those with both powers very common in Africa?"

"No, they are not," Chulaika replied. "In truth, only in recent generations have people with any kind of power become commonplace. As recently as in my great-grandmother's day, even my meager powers would have been cause for my people to shun me as a witch. But today a very powerful witch-queen sits upon the throne in Johara. Such powers are the only thing that people now respect."

"Perhaps," Wulfston said, "and perhaps not. Among my people there is the legend of another Wulfston—Wulfston the Red. He had no powers, yet he is remembered as a great ruler. His strength came from his unselfish love for his people, which earned him their respect and loyalty. Surely your history also contains stories of great kings and queens who ruled the Zionae without powers."

"Indeed," Chulaika nodded, "but those were in the days when Movers were few. In recent generations leaders without powers have had to fight constantly to keep their thrones. Of late, few have succeeded."

The Lord Adept shrugged. "A ruler's lands are his only for as long as he can hold them. There will always be someone wanting to make those lands his own, and having powers will never change that. You have seen our solution in the Savage Empire, Chulaika. Rulers who respect and trust one another can unite to maintain peace. Without that unity, powers or no powers, no ruler's lands are safe."

"Perhaps," she whispered. Wulfston could not tell whether she doubted his words, or found a seed of hope in them.

The cry of "Land ho!" rang out from the bow, and the passengers rushed to the rails for the first view of something other than water and sky since they had sailed out of the midland sea and into open ocean. A wide patch of green was slowly rising from the sea.

"Freedom Island," Chulaika identified. "We must stop there for water and supplies. After that, it is four more days until we reach the African coast."

Wulfston glanced at Captain Laren, who confirmed her words with a nod.

"Why is it called Freedom Island?" Zanos asked Chulaika.

"Because it is the last hope of slaves who sometimes manage to jump overboard after a slave ship has left Africa's west coast, bound for distant markets."

Like the Aventine Empire, Wulfston reflected, *until the last earthquake destroyed their system of rule, and we took over.*

"Many of the enslaved come from conquered tribes," Chulaika went on. "Thus they have no home to return to. So they stay on Freedom Island, joining one of the communities there. Pirate bands also use the island as a base, but it is unwritten law that no slave business is conducted here."

"And all those different factions live side by side in peace?" Astra asked.

"An uneasy peace," the veiled woman said. "Most uneasy."

No other ships were in the harbor when the *Night Queen* dropped anchor. Captain Laren and several of her crew went ashore first for supplies, and the boat returned for Wulfston, Zanos, Astra, Chulaika, and Chaiku.

Chulaika tried to persuade Wulfston to remain aboard, insisting, "There is nothing of interest to you on that island."

That only made him more certain there was, so he told her, "You said you would be my teacher as well as my guide. Here is my first chance to see African culture—and I need you to explain it to me." *Besides,* he thought, *I must attempt to send a message to Aradia.*

When Chulaika still resisted, Wulfston demanded, "What are you afraid of? Is there some danger on the island?"

"I cannot be certain," she replied. "I have never been here before. Although it is said that there is little violence on Freedom Island, you may be certain that should we encounter trouble, we can expect no help from the inhabitants."

Zanos gave her a confident smile. "I think we have enough strengths and talents among us to handle any trouble."

His wife nodded her agreement, but asked Chulaika, "Just what is it you fear? Surely Z'Nelia's influence could not reach so far."

"Couldn't it?" the African woman countered. "She has spies everywhere on the continent. Why not here?"

The handful of black people on the dock proved less than friendly, though not openly hostile to the strangers. To test whether he would be understood, Wulfston asked to have the letter he had prepared sent back on the next ship to the Aventine peninsula. He handed over coins, hoping the missive would reach its destination. Then they went on to the marketplace.

The half-mile walk was on a well-worn road lined with squalid huts. Children played in the dirt, while their mothers clustered nearby in the shade of a tall tree. It was of a type Wulfston did not recognize, and sitting in its branches were multicolored birds singing unfamiliar songs. *More than just another land,* he reflected. *It's almost like entering another world.*

The group of native women stopped talking as they passed, staring at the strangers—no, staring directly at him.

"Astra," Wulfston murmured in the savage language, "why are those women looking at me that way?"

The Reader followed his gaze and concentrated. "They're low-level Readers, my lord. My impression is that they are intrigued with your appearance, and are wondering who you— Oh, Hesta!" she muttered, and turned away, blushing.

"What's wrong?"

Zanos, who had apparently been "listening in" on his wife's scan of the women, choked back laughter. "Uh . . . they're Reading through your clothes, Lord Wulfston."

Fighting the reflex to cover himself with his hands, Wulfston gasped, "What!" then forced himself to walk tall, shooting an angry glare at the women that would have sent any citizen of his own land scurrying away in terror. The result on the group of women, however, was an explosion of laughter.

"They're breaking the Reader's Code!" he protested to Astra.

"They would be in the Savage Empire," she agreed, "but who knows whether in this part of the world Readers have even developed a code?"

They switched back to Chulaika's native language, and Astra asked her about it. "Each order of Seers has its own rules," the African woman explained. "I'm sure those women belong to no order, but even if they did, I doubt that our Seers and Movers could ever agree on a single set of rules.

We are too many different tribes and peoples, as you will soon see."

The marketplace was a sprawling arena of bustling activity, its perimeters defined by merchants' huts, tents, and open-air booths. Although it was not as crowded as a busy market day at home, the travelers found it difficult to navigate the crosscurrents of people.

Everyone seemed to travel in groups, as if being alone were unacceptable here. Or dangerous.

Wulfston noticed that the business being conducted did not involve the exchange of coins, only barter. Of course, refugees would not have silver or gold. Coins marked merchants, always under suspicion of trading in human flesh.

Wulfston touched the money pouch at his belt, and suddenly felt more an intruder on this island than a visitor. He felt even less certain that his letter would reach Aradia.

Zanos said, "The market seems to be divided into territories." Wulfston saw what he meant: tall, thin men sold their wares in the northern part; short, almost childlike people on the east—

But it was a small booth on the southern perimeter that drew Wulfston's attention. A young couple were selling wooden utensils. The man was beardless, but still he closely resembled the Lord Adept in build and skin color.

He reminds me of my father, Wulfston realized. His natural father. No, on closer examination this man didn't really look like his father as Wulfston remembered him, but there was family—tribal?—resemblance enough to give him the irrational feeling that if he walked over to that booth he would be welcomed with open arms.

Knowing his perception was clouded by memory, Wulfston remained where he was, letting his eyes move over to the man's wife, who was light-skinned and very pretty. She was painting animal figures on the outer edge of a large bowl, just as Wulfston's mother had done at his family's pottery stand. Over to the side a little girl was watching her young brother, a boy no more than three years old—

The same age I was when it all happened. It's like looking at my own past!

The young woman glanced in his direction, and her eyes widened. She edged over to the man and whispered something, then went to bend over her children.

A hand touched Wulfston's shoulder. He turned reflexively, staring into Chulaika's eyes, but he could not seem to hear what she was saying. His mind was still on the family that looked so much like his own. When he turned to look again, they were gone. The booth was empty.

"Lord Wulfston," Chulaika said, "Zanos claimed he saw some 'Madurans' over there"—she gestured toward the western side of the square—"and ran off. His wife followed him. She seems concerned. These 'Madurans'—they are his tribe?"

Wulfston nodded. "It never occurred to me that enslaved Madurans could end up this far south."

"That is the essence of the slave business," Chulaika said quietly. "People are sold in lands far from their homes, places where their features are considered unusual. They don't know the language, they stand out in a crowd, so there is little chance of escape."

Suddenly she looked around. "Chaiku? Chaiku!" Her eyes were suddenly wide with panic.

"He's just wandered off," Wulfston said, trying to see through the river of people flowing around them.

"Chaiku!" she called, her voice quickly approaching hysteria. "Chaiku!"

"Don't worry," he said firmly. "We'll find him. He can't have gone far."

But Chulaika continued to call her son, pushing her way through the crowd. Wulfston followed her, certain the little boy would wander back to where he had started.

"KANA LA SABENU Z'NELIA! KANA LA SABENU Z'NELIA!"

The shouts cut through every other sound in the square.

The world went silent for a moment, everyone looking in every direction at once. Then a woman yelled something and people scurried away from the center of the marketplace.

It was as though curtains parted, revealing little Chaiku—index finger in mouth, cheeks stained with tears—looking around bewilderedly for his mother.

And then the crowds parted further to reveal the screaming man, several yards beyond the child and lurching toward him with a drunken stagger.

He was brandishing a knife!

"KANA LA SABENU Z'NELIA!"

By now, Chulaika had reached her son and was scooping him up in her arms. Wulfston ran toward them, shouting for her to get out of the way as the man increased speed and raised the dagger.

Chulaika stood frozen, staring at her oncoming death.

The Lord Adept jumped to his right to see his target clearly, and threw enough Adept force to knock the knife out of the man's hand.

It was as though the attacker had been thrown against a stone wall—bones snapped loudly, the knife went flying behind him, and his shouts became a groaning gurgle as he dropped to his knees. He fell forward, to land at Chulaika's feet.

"Are you all right?" Wulfston asked as he approached her. She nodded vaguely, staring down at the man. Her right hand held Chaiku's face buried in her left shoulder, muffling his frightened sobs. Her eyes held an expression Wulfston could not discern, a strange mixture of fear and anger.

Suddenly Zanos and Astra were there, she kneeling over the prone form, he protectively standing over her and scanning the curious onlookers. "He's dead, Wulfston," she announced, looking up at him sadly. "His neck is broken."

"I didn't mean to strike him so hard," he muttered, fighting down a sick feeling. He hadn't misgauged his powers that badly since adolescence. He looked at Chulaika. "What was he shouting?"

She blinked. "Death to the enemies of Z'Nelia."

"Lord Wulfston, I think we should return to the ship," Astra said as she rose. "I don't like what I'm Reading from this crowd."

"I agree," Chulaika said quickly. "This man may have friends."

Wulfston had to agree. He let Zanos lead the way out of the marketplace, hand on the hilt of his sword.

The trek back was long and silent. Only when the ship was in sight did Wulfston relax enough to ask Zanos about the Madurans he had sought in the marketplace.

"There's a small colony of them on the island," Zanos replied quietly. "A storm enabled them to escape the ship carrying them to the mainland slave markets. Since no ships from here travel to Madura anymore, they are cut off from their homeland. Considering what Astra and I saw of Madura under Maldek's rule, I told them it's just as well."

Captain Laren and some of his crewmen were loading supplies, and the *Night Queen* put out to sea before night-fall. Wulfston gathered Zanos, Astra, and Huber for a private conference in the cramped quarters that were the only private accommodation available to the Lord Adept.

Astra used her powers to make sure no one was eavesdropping—particularly Chulaika.

"I'm even more suspicious of that woman now," Wulfston said tightly. "All her answers seem to be truthful, but something tells me that what she does *not* say is much more important than the information she's given us."

"Well," Astra said doubtfully, "I don't think she could have lied about what that man with the knife was saying. He was obviously out to kill Chaiku, Chulaika, and you."

"Perhaps he was a hired assassin," Huber suggested, "sent by Z'Nelia."

"If he was," Zanos commented, "he was a poor choice. It's very hard to sneak up on prey when you're drunk."

"Besides, no one knew we would stop on Freedom Island," said Wulfston. "No—wait. Sukuru and his people knew we would stop there because they did."

"Could Z'Nelia's allies have captured them?" Zanos mused. "Made them reveal that we were coming?"

Huber doubted it. "Even if someone Read it from them, Sukuru and his crew are only a day or so ahead of us. We're still four days from Africa—not enough time to put an assassin on the island."

"Unless he was already there," said Astra. "And what if he was a Reader himself? These people have no Code to stop them from invading people's privacy. If that man picked up Chulaika's thoughts and realized that she was Z'Nelia's enemy, he could have attacked her without thinking. Maybe he was just drunk enough not to realize he had no chance against us."

Wulfston said, "If that's so, then I'm even more worried. An ally or servant of Z'Nelia's so far from the mainland . . . just how far does her power extend?"

The language lessons continued, but Wulfston found it harder to concentrate. And he did not sleep well.

On the third morning, Zanos said to him, "You're like the fighters I used to train for the Aventine arena. Some of them would be restless for days before an important match."

"And how did you help them relieve their tensions?" Wulfston asked.

"Sometimes," the Maduran said wryly, "I'd send them to Morella's House of Pleasure."

Wulfston gave him a look of mock annoyance. "I don't think that applies here."

Zanos chuckled. He knew the Lord Adept was virgin-sworn until he found the woman who would provide his heir. "Sorry. Seriously, though, you need to get your mind off what lies ahead. When they were too tense, I would often set my gladiators a new challenge, something they'd never done before. For example, you are a power-ful Adept. I might challenge you to combat, with the stipulation that you not use your powers to win."

Wulfston looked at the powerfully muscled Maduran. As an Adept, he much overmatched Zanos, but without the use of powers— "I wouldn't know where to begin. I've never even learned to use a sword."

"I had to keep my powers secret in the Aventine Em-pire," said the ex-gladiator, "so I had to learn."

"Perhaps you should teach me swordplay," said Wulfston. "I may well have to hide my identity in order to get close enough to rescue Lenardo."

"No," replied Zanos. "The sword has many forms, each with its own style of combat. I could not possibly teach you enough in a few days to do you any good. But there is something that is useful anywhere in the world: the tactics of hand-to-hand combat."

Wulfston stared. "Wrestling? With *you*?" Zanos must weigh at least a third more than he did. "Without Adept powers I'd never dare come within reach of an enemy of your size!"

The Maduran's massive chest muscles rippled with his laughter. "I'll show you some tricks of combat strategy and the use of strength. Like you, I've learned to work with nature. But Adept combat sometimes goes against that principle."

"You mean because most Adept combat is a matter of powers and stamina. Drain your enemy's strength before he can drain yours."

"Exactly. Novices in the wrestling pit think the same way: wear down your opponent with brute force. But the seasoned fighters learn to turn an opponent's weight and strength against him. Let me demonstrate . . . Ho there, Telek!" he called to a tall, muscular deckhand who was watching from near the stern. "I've heard you're pretty good at fighting."

The crewman gave Zanos a lazy smile. "I've been in a brawl or two," he conceded, casually moving toward the gladiator.

Wulfston did not have to be a Reader to sense the anticipation rippling through the crew and some of the other passengers. Like the Lord Adept, many of them had noticed the looks of appraisal passing between Zanos and Telek. As the two largest men aboard, strangers to each other, it would be natural for them to speculate. Zanos did it out of habit, since judging men in the gladiatorial arena had been part of his profession.

Telek's reasons were another matter entirely. Wulfston had overheard several crewmen boast about his fighting prowess.

"I need your help to show something to Lord Wulfston," Zanos said to him. "Just some basic fighting moves."

Wulfston did not much care for the oily smile that Telek gave in response, but he remained silent as Astra appeared at his elbow. The Reader's confident smile told him to trust Zanos.

In size and musculature, the two men were almost identical. Telek's deeply bronzed skin and sun-bleached hair contrasted, though, with Zanos' exotic coloring. The sailor stripped off his shirt, cast it aside, and stretched.

The two men faced off, each taking a basic wrestler's stance. A ring of spectators formed around them as the fighters began circling. After several feints, they smashed together, each seeking a superior hold. Telek found it first, twisted his huge bulk, and tossed Zanos over his right hip.

Laughter erupted from some of the crewmen as the gladiator crashed to the deck. Wulfston saw Astra blink hard.

"That was what you had in mind, gladiator?" Telek smirked.

Zanos rose deliberately, smiling. Telek took two steps
and tried to grasp Zanos' arm. In a blur of speed, the
gladiator grabbed the sailor's wrist, spun around, and threw
Telek over his shoulder. Several crewmen jumped out of
the way as their comrade landed so hard the ship rocked.

"*That's* what I had in mind," Zanos said calmly. Wulfston
followed his gaze to Captain Laren, who was feigning
disinterest in the demonstration. The Lord Adept sensed
that the captain disapproved, but would allow them to
continue . . . within limits.

Telek bounced to his feet, no longer smug. He approached Zanos a little more cautiously—but soon found
himself flat on the deck again. This time a cheer went up
for Zanos.

Telek scrambled to his feet, glaring. Zanos' smile became nasty as he backed away, beckoning to his opponent.
Telek charged, bellowing. Zanos evaded his grasp, gripped
the seaman's forearms, planted his foot on Telek's chest,
and fell backward, tossing the man over his head.

The ship had stopped rocking before Telek regained his
feet this time. Zanos stood waiting. Silence fell on the
Night Queen as the two men stared at one another.

Suddenly Telek let out a long, hearty laugh, breaking
the tension. Zanos grinned as the sailor threw him a
careless salute and walked away, retrieving his shirt as he
went.

Someone tossed Zanos a towel as the circle of spectators
dispersed. Wiping the sheen of sweat from his torso, he
said, "You see, my lord? I used his own weight against
him, so I didn't wear myself out. If that principle could be
used in Adept combat, a man could fight much more
efficiently, without risking exhaustion."

"But both of you were using Adept powers, weren't
you?" Wulfston guessed. "Just before that last toss, Telek
braced his powers, and you countered with yours." Wulfston
could not have explained how he knew that, except from
years of experience with Adepts of all levels of ability.

"Zanos, what was the real point of that demonstration—to find out which of you was the better fighter?" To Wulfston it appeared that this skilled gladiator had lowered himself to brawl with a common thug.

Zanos shrugged. "It seemed the perfect opportunity to get that question answered."

"But was it important to do so?" Wulfston asked.

"Yes," was Zanos' only response. "Let's go back to where we started, my lord. With the same basic techniques, you could take on someone even larger than me without using Adept power."

Wulfston was still skeptical, but willing to take Zanos' instruction. However, he had to ask, "How do we keep each other honest about not using our powers?"

"I will referee," said Astra. "The moment either one of you braces his powers, he becomes unReadable—and I call foul."

Zanos limited the lesson to using an opponent's weight against him. Wulfston learned how to throw a man over his shoulder. But first, denied the use of his powers, he discovered how it felt to be the one thrown.

Twice he lunged at Zanos, trying to get a grip on the gladiator—and twice he was flipped so easily that he could not believe Zanos used no more than physical skill.

"When you lose the advantage," Zanos explained as Wulfston discovered the sting of bruises where he hadn't known he had places to bruise, "you roll away from the blow, or from the throw. Don't let the momentum go into impact. Keep rolling and it won't hurt so much. It also gives you time to gather your wits and find a new advantage."

"I'll remember that," said Wulfston as he struggled to his feet for the third time, feinted a stagger—and threw his shoulder into Zanos' knees, toppling the bigger man full length on the deck.

Zanos rolled to his feet, laughing. "You're an apt pupil, my lord! I'll make the lesson a little harder tomorrow."

*   *   *

The next morning Wulfston awoke to a new awareness of his body. It was not just the minor aches and bruises that persisted despite his use of healing power. Somehow he also felt refreshed and relaxed. The morning's language lesson went well, and he found himself looking forward to another session of training with Zanos in the afternoon.

But that was forgotten when Astra announced, "My lord! I can Read the shoreline of Africa!"

"What do you see?" Wulfston asked. "Can you find Sukuru's ship?"

"Perhaps," she replied, "but it would speed my search to know where the ship might be anchored."

Captain Laren unfurled his maps, Chulaika at his side. She pointed out a small port called Bosa. "Our journey to your land began from there, most excellent lord. But I doubt that the ship will still be anchored there, if Sukuru and the others have gone ashore."

"And why is that?"

"Her captain fears your wrath, and will flee as soon as Sukuru releases him."

Zanos let out an exasperated snort. "And Sukuru will certainly move Lenardo inland, no matter where they landed. So how do we decide where to start our search?"

"Let me go out of body," said Astra. "Perhaps I can locate Lord Lenardo."

"But the ship is moving," said Wulfston. "Will you be able to find your way back to your body?"

Zanos said, "I'll be her anchor. We have a strong mental rapport. Because of that, even my limited powers are enough to guide Astra back, no matter how far she roams."

As husband and wife shared a look of confirmation, Wulfston glimpsed in their eyes a special joy such as had never been a part of his life. For one brief moment a pang of jealousy touched him, but he dismissed it, bracing his Adept powers to guard Astra's body should her Reading be discovered by somebody ashore.

* * *

Astra's spirit was gone from her body for almost an hour. When she opened her eyes, she reported that Sukuru and his people had indeed been put ashore at Bosa. And the ship was gone.

"Lord Lenardo was unconscious when they took him off the ship," Astra reported. "From what I could Read of the local residents, Sukuru must have told them we're in pursuit of him—and very angry. They're deserting the area in terror."

"It is as Sukuru planned it," Chulaika stated. "You will find no one to help you in your search for Lord Lenardo."

"Then we'll do without the help of others," Wulfston replied. "One way or another, our search will soon be over."

A short time later, the African coastline came into view. Wulfston found Astra alone at the port rail, staring at the land. He approached hesitantly, drawn by a feeling of concern.

"May I ask what you are thinking, Astra?"

"I . . . I know this may sound strange," the Reader responded, "but this view of the coastline reminds me of my first view of Madura. The two don't look anything alike." She glanced up at some black birds soaring overhead. "Even the birds are different. But all the memories of what happened there suddenly came flooding back to me."

"That doesn't sound strange at all," Wulfston assured her. "From what little I've heard of that journey, you faced hostile forces at every turn. We may have to face even worse dangers here, Astra. But . . . would it be prying to ask what happened in Madura? What Zanos found in his homeland?"

She considered. "Zanos doesn't like to talk about Madura because the journey became such a disappointment. After more than twenty years of struggle and heartache, he

finally found his brother Bryen. The only member of
Zanos' family left alive, and within days he, too, was
dead."

She turned to look into Wulfston's eyes. "All the years
that Zanos was trapped in the Aventine Empire, he was
sustained by his dream of returning home, taking with
him all the Aventine slaves who wanted to live as free men
in Madura. But Vortius the Gambler destroyed his plans
to help the slaves escape, and when Zanos finally reached
his homeland he found that the sorcerer Maldek had turned
Madura into a place of ugliness and sterility. A land of
death.

"So Zanos' dreams all ended in frustration. He doesn't
talk about them anymore, but I know—"

She stopped, her eyes taking on the unfocused look of a
Reader concentrating completely on Reading, to the ex-
clusion of her immediate surroundings.

At the same time, Wulfston shuddered. Something was
wrong. It took him a moment to realize that it was the
silence. The birds had stopped their harsh cries, the creak-
ing of the ship's timbers had ceased, and the sails no
longer flapped against the rigging.

The silence lasted hardly long enough for him to recognize it before a sound came out of the distance—a wind,
rapidly building to a gale!

The *Night Queen* pitched and swayed as choppy waves
drove against it, then huge breakers slammed the hull as
the wind tore at the sails.

This is no work of nature! Wulfston realized.

"An Adept wind?" Astra answered his unspoken thought.

"It has to be!" he replied, shouting over the increasing
howl. He had no need to raise his voice for the Readers,
but: "Captain Laren! It's not just a storm! We're under
attack!"

As the sailors scrambled to haul in the sails before the
ship capsized, Astra exclaimed, "I can't find the source,

my lord! The Adepts are beyond my range. I'll have to go
out of body to search."

"Too dangerous," he responded. White clouds were churn-
ing into black thunderheads. Bracing his powers, Wulfston
prepared himself for battle against an unseen enemy.

Zanos fought his way to them against the wind, and put
a protective arm around his wife's shoulders. "My lord,"
he shouted, "we must combine our powers to combat this
storm!"

"We have to try!" Wulfston agreed. "Unless we can
locate the source, the best we can do is shield ourselves
and try to get the ship out of range."

They had to struggle for every step to the center of the
deck. The first bolt of lightning struck the top of the
mainmast, exploding it into splinters. The Adepts deflected the falling shards from passengers and crew, but
the ship was hopelessly crippled. They were trapped!

"Support me!" Wulfston commanded the minor Adepts,
and felt their power flow to him. With increased strength,
he fended off the next shaft of lightning. *But we cannot
keep this up indefinitely.*

"Where's Chulaika?" he demanded. "She might know
where the Adepts are gathered to attack us."

But Chulaika was not on deck. Captain Laren was shouting to his men to lower the sails on the surviving masts,
while the steersman hauled hopelessly on the rudder,
trying to keep a southward course. Captain Laren reached
for the rudder, to add his strength—and another thunderbolt turned him to a pillar of fire!

Wulfston recoiled in momentary horror as the corpse
was pitched from the heaving deck.

Fireballs rained on the ship.

Wulfston felt his powers drain as he deflected them.

A wave of flame broke through their shield, death screams
erupting around him as he was knocked to his hands and
knees.

A lightning bolt sliced through the deck in front of him—the last sight he saw as the brightness blinded him.

There has to be a way to fight back! his mind insisted, but he was helpless, blind, unable to get back on his feet as he heard people screaming around him, smelled the stench of burning flesh.

He groped, found a handhold on one of the small boats, and hauled himself to his feet as his vision began to return from the edges inward.

It was just in time to see Zanos rolling Astra on the deck, smothering the flames from her dress.

Bodies were burning, ropes were flaring, sailors were hauling buckets of seawater to pour over the writhing form of a man screaming as his flesh was consumed.

Wulfston put out that fire and sent the man into healing sleep, but even as he did so he felt his growing weakness and saw how hopeless his small efforts were. He turned to help Zanos and Astra—

The deck exploded under him, tossing him high into the air before dropping him amid the rest of the debris in the roiling madness of the storm-wild ocean.

Chapter Three

*G*asping for breath, Wulfston felt the surf carry him toward the beach, but a powerful undertow swept him back to sea again. He struggled to pull air into his burning lungs, and took in a mouthful of sea and sand.

Another surge swept him toward shore, but pulled him under and rolled him in a helpless tangle. As it retreated he felt sand beneath him, and thrust his feet down. The wave carried his purchase from beneath him, but his feet sank ankle-deep in the shifting sand.

Lurching to his knees, he wheezed, the water a cold ache in his lungs, closing out the air. But there was land under him!

He forced gritty eyes open and saw the beach, stumbled toward it pursued by another voracious wave, and fell on his face at the edge of the water.

For an endless time he coughed and vomited sand and seawater, leaving his throat and nasal passages raw. When the spasms finally passed, he was weak and sick . . . and alone.

His eyes still burned, but he could open them. To the west was the empty sea, all traces of the *Night Queen* swallowed in its depths save for black smoke drifting toward the clearing horizon. The tide retreated in a steady ebb and flow. North and south stretched the beach, with no signs of life except three little brown birds following the edges of the waves back and forth, snatching exposed edibles.

To the east stood a forest, impenetrable as a solid wall. It lined the beach in both directions, as far as he could see, unfamiliar and forbidding. But unless he found a stream running down to the shore he would have to go inland to search for fresh water.

When he could stand, Wulfston assessed himself. He was bruised and aching, but in the uncertainty of what lay ahead, he dared not waste energy healing such minor ills. He seemed to have no broken bones, but when he tried to walk his feet responded with sharp pain.

Wulfston quickly discovered the problem: he was wearing hose, a silk shirt, and a lightweight tabard that was now soggy and uncomfortable. His hose had been torn in the surf, and a few recalcitrant threads clung between his bare toes, cutting into the tender flesh. He reached for his knife, but it was gone. Picking up a broken shell, he cut off the hose at his ankles, leaving his feet bare.

From the calves upward, although they bore holes, his hose were in good enough condition to provide some warmth against the coming night. He took them off, along with the tabard, letting the shirt dry on his body. Ordinarily he would have had everything dry with a thought; alone and exposed, he feared to waste what power he had left on mere comfort.

Above the tideline, the sand was dry. Wulfston laid tabard and hose out there; they couldn't get any sandier than they already were. The waves had driven sand into every pore and crevice of his body.

It was warm enough to go without even the shirt, but although there was no one in sight, he felt defenseless enough without stripping naked. Modesty was better served, though, by turning the shirt into a makeshift loincloth.

Remembering the women Reading through his clothes on Freedom Island, he wondered if anyone were Reading him now, or even watching from the dense forest. He couldn't worry about that. He had to try to find survivors of the shipwreck.

He wondered whether he should try north or south, until he remembered that Chulaika had said the harbor Sukuru had used was to the south.

Surviving Readers would be scanning for him—for anyone who had reached shore. Further reason not to use his Adept powers: they made him unReadable except to visualization, a technique a weary Reader would not be using after the battle with the sea.

So he picked up his soggy clothes and trudged down the beach, keeping as far as he could manage from the edge of the threatening forest.

Before he had gone half a mile, his feet were cut and bleeding from sharp shell fragments buried in the sand. He cursed himself for kicking his boots off in the sea—but they had filled with water and weighed him down. Rather than risk infection, he used healing power to close the cuts, and continued on his way.

Up ahead, he saw a shape at the edge of the water—a survivor! He broke into a run, but the man didn't stir. When Wulfston touched him, he knew at once that he was dead; the body was cold and stiff, already starting to bloat.

Wulfston turned the man over, and recognized one of the *Night Queen* sailors, one rigid hand gripping a piece of railing. Should he use the strength needed to create a funeral pyre—white heat to return the body properly to the elements? The man's clothes were so wet—

And, sturdy workman's garments, they were in much better condition than Wulfston's.

He was uneasy at the thought of robbing the dead, yet this man had no further use for that heavy seaman's shirt and those thick-soled shoes that might well have been what pulled him under and drowned him.

I will give him a proper funeral pyre in exchange for what he can no longer use, Wulfston decided, and bent to the task of stripping the rigid corpse.

But the moment he began to move the body, a shout rang out from the edge of the forest.

Wulfston looked up.

A dozen men ran toward him, armed with knives, spears, and clubs.

Like Wulfston, they were naked except for a covering about their loins, but they wore chains of what appeared to be bones about their necks.

Other than that, they wore only headbands, all alike, each with the same symbol in bright beadwork. They charged down the beach, then paused to throw their spears—and Wulfston saw a weapon new to him.

What had appeared to be a spear was actually made of two pieces. When a man flung one, he kept the heavier lower end in his hand, while something like a long, heavy arrow shot forth with the strength of his swing and whizzed toward Wulfston!

He used his powers to deflect the arrows, but his attackers kept coming.

He sent a sheet of flame leaping before the startled band, but the moment it disappeared they charged toward him. As they spread out in a semicircle, Wulfston knew he had made a mistake in giving his Adept powers away. They knew how to take an Adept: divide his attention and make him use up his strength.

If his powers had been at full strength, he might have withstood them. But at twelve to one, given his current condition, he had no choice but to run.

He darted to the right, angling up the sand, abandoning his bundle of clothes beside the drowned sailor.

Using Adept power to strengthen his tired legs, he plunged through the dry sand at the top of the beach, deflecting the spear-arrows that pursued him.

One of the men was fast enough to catch him. He felt a hand on his arm, turned, and saw the upraised club. He stopped the man's heart. His attacker fell, pulling Wulfston down with him in his death spasm.

Wulfston peeled the dead man's fingers away and sprinted

for the forest, Adeptly forcing his lungs to take in air, his limbs to move in rhythm.

He plunged into a different world!

This forest was like none he had ever known. It was jungle, as thick with undergrowth as with trees. He staggered and slid on rotted vegetation, blinded by the difference between the hot yellow beach and this dark greenness where the sun could hardly penetrate. Birds screamed at his noisy passage, and small animals fled through the trees.

The air was cool and moist, a relief to his aching lungs, but the smell was frighteningly different from any he had ever known.

To avoid his pursuers, he zigzagged through the trees. The jungle would not let him choose his own path, but made him go where it provided openings. Over and over he found his way blocked by roots, rocks, thickets.

He ran until he could run no further. Exhausted, he leaned against the sloping trunk of a huge tree, gasping for breath. The jungle had fallen silent.

Through the roaring in his ears, he listened for pursuit. There was nothing. As his breathing calmed, he realized that it was too silent around him. The jungle was watching this intruder like a cat, waiting for the right moment to pounce.

He was lost.

Sunlight filtered through dappled green shade, diffused so that he could not tell what direction it came from, nor could he hear the pounding of the surf. He didn't know how to get back to the beach—and if he could, would those warriors be waiting for him?

He needed rest, but first he needed food. In the woods near where he had grown up, he would have been able to put together a meal in minutes; here he could see berries, fungus, some yellow fruit on a nearby tree . . . but which of it was safe, and which poisonous?

Besides, he needed meat to restore his strength. And he was desperately thirsty.

His heart stopped pounding in his ears, and his breathing returned to a rapid but normal pace. Through the silence he heard a soft rushing; it had to be water.

Pushing himself away from the support of the tree, he moved toward the sound, pausing often to listen, following as the sound became slowly louder until he came out at a pool into which a small cascade fell from a rocky but overgrown hillside.

With no thought except slaking his thirst, Wulfston rushed to the pool, sinking calf-deep into mud among the rushes that lined it, and on into the water itself.

It was cold and clear. He sank into it, drank it in, let it wash away salt and sand and sweat.

But it was too cold to stay in. He swam to the rock wall and pulled himself out onto a secure perch, where he sat and watched for fish to return to feeding now that the disturbance was gone. He knew that it was safe to eat any scaly fish, and he hoped that he still had enough strength to kill a fish and make a fire to cook it.

A wave of hunger swept through him as he thought about grilling fish. His mouth watered.

But the fish stayed out of sight.

He would have to call them, his desperate need for food outweighing his reluctance to lure a creature only to kill it.

This ability to influence animals had been the first Adept power Wulfston had manifested, when he was three years old. He had used it for amusement then, calling rabbits and squirrels to play with him, to the delight of the other village children. Over the years he had used it to calm frightened horses, or wounded animals so he could heal them.

Now, though, he had no choice but to use it to feed himself. He felt more naked without the full strength of his powers than without his clothes.

He began to picture the pool from beneath the water, where he had been a few minutes before. He thought of a big, fat fish wanting to go up toward the surface, where there was food.

Sure enough, just such a fish swam lazily to the dappled surface of the pool. Wulfston began to lure it closer, giving it the desire to come within his grasp. When it was just below the rock on which he perched, he stopped its heart quickly, painlessly, and reached down—

Wulfston got a fleeting impression of something with teeth enough for an army as the fish was snatched away!

He started back, fear tingling through his nerves and emerging from his skin in cold sweat.

There was a monster in the pool!

He stared as the thing resurfaced, a lizardlike animal as large as a man, with a back like a log, a tapering tail that moved lazily to rudder it through the water, and a head that was ugliness personified. Eyes atop the head stared coldly at him, defying him to dare try again for its prey, but it was the creature's snout that held his gaze. His impression of endless teeth was verified—there were so many that the mouth could not contain them all, and they snaggled in sharp array around the outside of the vicious maw.

Hungry and tired, Wulfston shivered uncontrollably with the realization that it could have been a part of his body, rather than that hapless fish, that made a meal for the water-beast. He had probably aroused it when he splashed unthinkingly into the pool. He had gotten out just in time! It could have attacked him while he was swimming, or just now it could have taken his hand.

Wulfston did not command the powers Zanos and Astra had seen in the frozen isles to the far north, where sorcerers knew how to make severed limbs regrow.

Dapples of yellow turned orange around the green pool, and Wulfston knew that soon the sun would set. He couldn't stay by the pool. Predators were likely to come to drink under cover of night, perhaps great cats that could see in the dark. He needed sleep. If there was to be no food, at least he could rest, and hunt again in the morning.

So with his stomach growling in protest, he set out in search of a safe place to sleep. Was there any safety for him here, in the land of his ancestors?

There was a cave in the rocky wall, bones, feathers, and bits of fur strewn on its floor. Wulfston could build a fire in the cave mouth, but once he fell into the virtual unconsciousness of Adept sleep he would not rouse to stoke the fire. It could go out, leaving him helpless before whatever had left those remains.

So he moved away from the pool, looking upward and wishing once again that he could Read. A perch in a tree was the only haven he could think of—provided he did not fall to his death in the night. To a Reader darkness was meaningless, and wild animals could be sensed at a distance and avoided. He *knew* the power was in him; Adept and Reading powers sprang from the same source. But there was no use now in grieving over his inability to manifest the other half of his talents.

In the dimming light, he saw a tree with wide, forking branches. The climb was not hard, and he found a place where he could wedge himself between a broad limb and the trunk of the tree, with a second limb beneath to catch him should he fall. It was not very comfortable, but he could not see the ground when he looked down. Predators relying on sight should not notice him.

If animals followed his scent, he could only hope that they were not the kind that climbed trees. Once he settled in one spot, it was hopeless to try to stay awake in the face of his body's need to restore itself.

Despite the hard, rough tree against his bare skin, he carefully arranged his body in the best compromise he could manage between safety and comfort. Wulfston felt himself sucked inexorably into the oblivion of Adept slumber.

Perhaps the gods would grant him protection for this one night—whatever gods held sway in this dark and alien land.

*   *   *

He was gorging on fresh meat, aware only of the smell
and taste, and the emptiness in his belly. The pack leaders
had brought down a water buffalo, and gorged their fill on
the smoking entrails and the liver, but there was meat
aplenty for the two young ones who now chewed on the
tough muscles, struggling even with their sharply pointed
teeth to tear off chunks to swallow whole, ready to run if—

Snarls warned him.

He saw the hyena coming up on the other side of the
carcass, warning him away.

But he was still hungry! He had had only a few mouth-
fuls! And his sister—

She was gone already, had turned and run from the
scavenger, knowing it perfectly capable of killing if it
wanted to.

For the first time in his life, hunger combined with
male instinct, and he stood his ground, his hackles rising,
growling in return, baring his teeth to show their sharp-
ness and the meat that was rightly his.

The hyena gave a bark of warning, and leaped over the
buffalo carcass.

The one eating growled in return, but the hyena thrust
its sharp nose under his tail, challenging.

He turned sharply, trying to do the same to the larger
beast, but the hyena went for his throat, tumbling the
younger animal head over heels in an attempt to escape
the slashing teeth.

Hunger made him brave. He got his feet under him and
leaped for the hyena's throat—but the larger animal was
wily and experienced. He caught the young dog by the
thick throat fur, shaking, trying to snap his neck.

This time youth and lack of experience overtook him—
when his opponent let go he cringed in fear, whining. The
hyena's wicked yellow teeth gashed his thigh. In response,
he turned on his back, belly exposed in submission.

The hyena snarled and threatened, standing between

the buffalo carcass and the dog, but he did not attack further.

The dog whined, then slunk off in the stink of his own blood and fear musk, his stomach still empty and protesting.

At the edge of the jungle his sister waited anxiously, crying, ready to lick his wounds—

Wulfston woke with a start, to full daylight. What a strange dream—he and Aradia as dogs—?

As he turned his stiff body to climb down the tree, Wulfston found himself eye to eye with the biggest snake he had ever seen. The body was wrapped around a branch above him, the head hanging down to peer at him from cold reptilian eyes.

Wulfston backed down the tree as hastily as he could without any sudden moves. His limbs were stiff from having remained in the same awkward position all night, but he didn't hurt. His body's healing powers had come automatically into play. But still his stomach demanded food.

He reached the foot of the tree and straightened, stretching his arms upward to ease his back—and his makeshift loincloth slid down to his ankles!

Wulfston picked up the silk shirt and unknotted it to retie it more securely about his loins. He knew what had happened: he had not provided his body with food to restore his strength, and so it had taken energy out of his own flesh.

He had to find food—his gut was aching. The fact that he was wide awake and feeling good except for the raging hunger told him that his powers were restored, but he could not use them without replacing the energy his body required. Adepts carried no extra body fat; the night's fast had taken all he could spare without giving up muscle.

He was still within the sound of the waterfall, so he went back, easily caught a fish and lifted it from the water with Adept power, and cooked it over a small fire he built on the rock ledge. He ate the first of it half raw, unable to wait for it to cook through.

When he had caught, cooked, and eaten a second fish, although he was not satisfied, he had at least given his body something to work with. He also felt more confident, now that he dared use his powers again.

Having fulfilled his first priority of nutrition, he had to decide what to do next. Surely the other survivors of the shipwreck were looking for him.

Were there other survivors? There had to be. Zanos and Astra would have combined their Adept powers to save themselves. And what about Chulaika and Chaiku? Sukuru had used them to bring Wulfston to Africa. Their usefulness over, had he discarded them? Or had they rejoined him?

He wasn't going to find them in the middle of the jungle. If he worked his way east for a few miles he would come out onto a plain—

How did he know that?

He realized the knowledge came from that weird dream, in which he and Aradia were half-grown wild dogs driven from their meal by a hyena.

Was that what the dream was really about? Or was that just the interpretation he had put on it when he woke up?

When he opened his mind to it, Wulfston realized that in the dream he had been the dog, not himself at all. The female had been sister, litter-mate, companion . . . but not Aradia.

It had been . . . real.

He had been in that dog's mind.

He had been . . . Reading?

Torio had once asked him how he knew where the animals were that he called. Had his defenseless state of last night dropped some barrier?

He sat beside the pool, and tried to Read. As always, nothing happened. Of course nothing happened. He'd had a dream, that was all!

So how did he know that a grassy plain lay beyond the jungle?

Well, how *did* he know? Maybe there was no plain.
Maybe there was nothing but more jungle, and if he went
east he would be farther and farther from any other survivors of the shipwreck. If he went west, he would certainly
come back to the ocean. But wouldn't the shore be where
Sukuru expected to find him? He had been attacked there
once already.

So . . . east or west?

And then, with chill prickles up his spine, he realized
that he *knew* east from west. He was no longer lost,
although the sun rode too high to be an indicator of
direction, and he had no lodestone. He just knew!

Something *had* happened to him in the night. Perhaps
it really was the opening of his Reading powers at last. He
had to find Astra—she'd quickly train him to use them.
But he had to keep from being captured or killed by
Sukuru, or by Z'Nelia's forces, who might assume he was
on Sukuru's side.

They knew he was not a Reader. They would assume
that, unable to traverse the jungle, and not knowing that
the plain lay within easy distance for an Adept, he would
go back to the sea.

Therefore he would go eastward, to the plain.

By high noon he came to the edge of the jungle. Before
him stretched the plain he had seen in his dream—grassland
as far as the eye could see, teeming with life.

Some animals he recognized—elephants were used for
heavy labor in the Aventine Empire, and lions had been
kept by the Emperor's family as if to demonstrate their
power by their hold on the king of beasts. But he did not
know the names of the many deerlike creatures, large and
small, some with horns that appeared too large for their
small heads to carry.

And the birds! Acres of flamingos turned the shore of a
lake a brilliant orangey-pink. Small brown birds hid in the
grass, while bright parrots perched in the occasional tree.
Crows and magpies lent their raucous cries to the snorts of

the lions and the trumpeting of the elephants, while above it all floated an eagle, watching with keen eyes for his prey.

In the grass, besides smaller birds there were mice and rabbits, little squirrellike animals, snakes, lizards and chameleons, insects.

The life of the plain called to something in Wulfston's blood. He was one with that community of nature under the open sky. It didn't even seem strange that he was seeing and hearing things too distant or too small and faint to perceive with his normal senses.

He knew what he had never consciously known before: his ancestors had come from here, from the plain, not from the jungle where enemies lurked. This . . . was home.

As if to reassure himself that he was not imagining his new senses, Wulfston became aware of two dogs—the young dogs of his dream. They were at the edge of the jungle, in the shade, the male lying down while the female licked at a nasty wound high on his left hind leg.

They were black, about half-grown. Wulfston understood they had been turned out of the pack to learn to fend for themselves, and would not be able to join another pack until they were grown. So they struggled to survive, their once happy rabbit-chasing no longer a game, but a deadly-earnest search for food.

Wulfston turned, and made out the two dogs because he knew where to look. They blended into the shadows, but he recognized that their black color would make them as conspicuous on the golden plain . . . as he was in the Savage Lands.

Using his power to make animals trust him, Wulfston walked toward the two dogs. When he came near, he saw that despite the way they had cleaned it with their tongues, the gash inflicted by the hyena's filthy teeth was starting to fester.

"Easy, boy," Wulfston murmured, offering his closed

hand to the male. The female bristled, and snarled at him from behind her brother.

But when the male sniffed his hand and accepted a pat on the head, Wulfston turned his attention to the young bitch and soon had her nuzzling his hand. He wished he had food to offer, but he was as hungry as they were.

When both dogs were calm, Wulfston laid his hand over the wound and sent healing heat to drive out the infection. He closed the wound from the inside out, while the female paced nervously and tried to shove her nose under his hand. When the healing was complete he let her, and watched both dogs sniff and lick the area where the wound had been, unable to understand where it had gone.

The male got up and tried his leg; he didn't limp at all. In a moment he was belly-down, hindquarters-up, inviting his sister to play.

Wulfston let the pups tumble for a few moments, then mentally called them to his side. "You," he told the male, "are Traylo, and you are Arlus," to the female, "and we are going to hunt some rabbits!"

Wulfston did the actual hunting, but the dogs didn't know that. When he called a rabbit from its burrow, Traylo and Arlus dashed after it. The rabbit tore off through the grass with the yipping dogs in hot pursuit.

But the object was food, not games. Before the rabbit could pop down another hole, Wulfston stopped its heart, then tried to control the dogs—

They were on their prey, hungry and victorious! Gleefully, they ripped into the warm, quivering flesh, fighting over the tender innards. Fur flew as they shredded the skin to reach the flesh, filling their bellies at last!

It was only when the dogs began to gnaw on the stripped bones that Wulfston came to himself, to the demands of his own empty stomach. He could smell and taste the raw meat, and the lingering memory when he withdrew forcefully from the dogs' perspective made him momentarily queasy.

Not for long, however; he had used what energy his early-morning meal had given him in healing Traylo, and his body once more clamored for food. Leaving the dogs to their prey, he caught and killed another rabbit, and soon had it spitted over a small fire.

Watching that the fire did not throw sparks into the grass, Wulfston pulled the outer flesh off the rabbit as it cooked, and ate while he considered what to do. Head toward that lake he had Read, for a drink of water. Perhaps he would find a trail there. Surely people would have settled along such a body of water, or would stop there on journeys across the plains. Perhaps he would find a trail leading south. To people.

He would have to approach people soon, if only to discover what fruits and vegetables he dared to eat in this land. Meat alone was inadequate nutrition, yet he feared to risk poison by eating the bright red berries that tempted him from a nearby thicket.

Traylo and Arlus came back. They accepted the bones from his rabbit, but buried them, as they were no longer hungry. Soon they were curled up together, fast asleep.

The more he thought, the more Wulfston realized that he could not avoid human habitation. Although his Adept powers allowed him to clean a rabbit without a knife, that was wasteful. And Adept or no, he had no way to carry water without some kind of container.

Zanos and Astra and the others would be looking for him in the settlements, too, not out on the plain. Yes, he would walk to the lake and see what trail he might pick up there.

Making certain the fire was out, Wulfston wrapped what was left of the rabbit in some leaves and set out. Traylo and Arlus trotted along beside him until his direction was established, then veered off after fascinating scents.

It was hot under the direct sun. Wulfston's black skin never burned like Aradia's fairness, but after a while he wished he had a covering for his head. The animals had

ceased their restless activity, spending the heat of the day
in burrows or in the shade of grass or thickets. Even the
herd animals lay down to rest in the hot afternoon glare.

Wulfston could see the lake ahead . . . or was it a
mirage formed by the waves of heat? He noticed the two
dogs now moving straight ahead, no more forays to either
side, and wondered if they could smell water.

With the thought, he was in their perceptions again,
scenting the welcome wetness, sharing their thirst. Their
keen noses told them far more than their eyes—they could
not see the zebra off to their left, but the not-quite-horse
smell was as clear as the smell inside a stable to Wulfston.

It didn't disturb Traylo and Arlus when Wulfston shared
their perceptions, so he remained within their minds, hearing the sounds of birds huddling down as the danger
passed, smelling a wider variety of scents than he had ever
imagined, but seeing little.

It wasn't just that the dogs' eyes were so close to ground
level; their *way* of seeing was different. There were not
nearly as many colors as Wulfston was used to, and everything was slightly out of focus.

With human instinct, he tried to see more clearly, but
the blur of tannish grass persisted. Suddenly there was a
movement ahead. A startled rodent dropped the stalk it
had been chewing on and scurried for its burrow, Arlus
and Traylo in hot pursuit.

There were two rodents, one to the left and one to the
right! He tried to turn toward one—then—

—tripped over a hummock and fell sprawling, the grass
giving way to let him hit the ground with a bruising
thump.

Back in his own senses, Wulfston realized what had
happened: he had been looking through both dogs' eyes at
once, each seeing the same rodent from a different
perspective.

He laughed as he picked himself up, and decided he
would not do that again—at least until he had had more

practice at watching where he was going while he Read something else!

Now he could definitely see the lake ahead. The dogs, having lost the little rodent, raced merrily into the shallow water and stopped to lap it up eagerly. Wulfston was not far behind them. He knelt, and dipped up water with his hands, then went in farther to cool off, trying to watch for dangerous animals as he splashed the water all over himself.

Feeling much better, he left the lake and began pacing along the shore, looking for a path that might indicate human use. All he saw were animal prints, and a flock of flamingos farther down the shoreline.

He couldn't believe people didn't come to this beautiful lake! Yet he saw no sign of villages or towns, no roads, no cultivated fields. He also saw no sheltered place where he could spend the night.

Although he was able to build a rapport with the animal life of the plain, the rodents and insects and little birds had no interest in man, except to avoid him. All he could tell was that there were no other people nearby; none of the animals gave him a perspective to tell whether there was a trail, even a road, beyond his line of sight.

Above the lake, however, soared a fish eagle, perhaps the same one he had seen in his first sensing of the lake that morning. *I wonder*— He hardly dared to think of it.

But that eagle could see the entire lake, and all the land surrounding it.

"Traylo! Arlus!" Wulfston called the dogs to him, and sat down cross-legged on the sandy shore.

The pups were wet, their fur standing up in points, and when they came to him they shook, spraying him with water. But they were panting, their tongues lolling out to give them a clownish look, and it was not hard to persuade them that they wanted to lie down next to him and groom their coats.

Even if the dogs fell asleep, they would be easily roused

and, should he succeed at his daring idea, would pull Wulfston's attention back at any sign of danger.

Readers and Adepts both learned relaxation and concentration exercises. Wulfston easily put himself into the quiet but ready state necessary for performing the most difficult and delicate of Adept functions, but instead of bracing himself to use those powers he let himself once again become attuned to the life about him. Slowly, hesitantly, he reached out to the eagle, trying to see what it saw.

Unlike the dogs, who welcomed his mental touch, the eagle merely *allowed* him to share its perceptions, and he sensed that it could and would drive him out if his presence became offensive. But all he wanted was to see—

—as he had never seen before!

The bird's vision was as much sharper than Wulfston's as his was than the dogs'!

As he floated on the currents of air, the world spread below in brilliant, sharply defined array. One of the little rodents skittered through the grass; silver-hued fish swam beneath the surface of the lake; frogs hopped from one lily pad to another along the far shore. Just north of the area where Wulfston had come to the lakeshore, a herd of water buffalo grazed, some of them standing knee-deep in the water, pulling up the lush green weeds.

At first Wulfston could do no more than marvel at the view, and at the sensation of floating above the world, divorced from its cares or pleasures. He was master of his world, untouchable in his high flight.

He thrilled to the sensation of tendon and muscle reacting to each shift in the wind, feathers spreading and retracting, the great wings held effortlessly open, supporting him easily. The bird spiraled slowly, sliding down an invisible column of air, then caught an updraft and rose again, triumphant in the sun's rays.

Wulfston had to struggle to make his own mind work, to look out the eagle's eyes but analyze with a man's mind. From here, his own path through the grassy plain was clear, as were the side trails the dogs had made. Their footprints along the lakeshore led as plainly as a cobbled street, and he could see himself, the dogs curled up on either side of him!

It was most disconcerting to observe his own body this way. He remembered Torio and Lenardo saying how disorienting it was, something belonging to the advanced stages of a Reader's training. But this was not the same thing as a Reader's visualizing. Their Code probably kept them from such a thing as looking through someone else's eyes.

Still, he wished the bird would not focus on him that way; it was strange to see that tired-looking, scruffy man wearing nothing but a fraying silk shirt turned into a loincloth, and realize that it was himself. From this vantage point, he was the least significant object in the landscape.

The bird began another slow downward spiral, and this time Wulfston was better able to keep his mind on observing. Sure enough, he saw what he was looking for: perhaps half a mile farther along the lakeshore there was an inlet, and from it a road stretched southward—a wagon track, clearly showing twin paths of the wheels, with the grass trying to survive between.

There was his road to human habitation! In fact, in the eagle's peripheral vision he thought he detected what might be man-made dwellings several miles away, but the bird would not oblige him by looking directly at them.

The eagle continued its lazy spiral, and Wulfston studied the landscape. There was more movement below— people on horses! They had intersected his trail from the south, and were turning to follow it toward the lake.

Who were they? //Look at them, eagle! Are they all black people, or are my white friends among them? Look there! I have to know!//

With a shock that sent spasms of pain wrenching through his head, Wulfston was back in his own body.

Resenting his demands, the eagle had dismissed him from its mind.

Taking only long enough to quell the pain, Wulfston climbed to his feet and ran back along his own trail. He was sure the horsemen were looking for him. But were they Sukuru's people, or Zanos and Astra?

Backtracking through the grass, Wulfston saw how easy he would be to follow—but perhaps they weren't expecting him to come to meet them. One thing concerned him: even on the edges of the eagle's peripheral vision, surely Zanos' bright red hair would have stood out, had the gladiator been there. Best consider these people his enemies until they proved otherwise.

He crouched, then crawled through the grass as he approached the area where he had seen the horsemen. Traylo and Arlus followed him, accepting him as pack leader and obeying his mental picture of them, staying close by his side until the danger was identified.

For the first time, he tried reaching out with his mind to Read people, but he got only a confused muddle. Astra, a Magister Reader, would surely not Read like that!

So he tried the horses. They were tired from a long ride, but aware of no strangers among the riders. So none of Wulfston's friends were there.

"Come on, Traylo, Arlus," he murmured, and started angling back toward the lake. It didn't matter if these were Sukuru's men or Z'Nelia's—he didn't want to be taken by either!

He could not tell whether he had been seen or Read, but a shout went up, and suddenly horses were galloping after him!

Not even an Adept could outrun a horse. He had to stand and fight.

There were nine of them, but no one shot an arrow or threw a spear at him this time. They spread out, and he saw nets unfurled. They wanted to capture, not kill him.

As the first rider approached, net spinning, Wulfston

grasped control of it and flung it back over the man's own head, tangling him in its folds.

While he struggled to free himself, though, the others spread in a circle around Wulfston.

He shot a lightning bolt searing the air before the nearest horse. The animal screamed and reared, but the grass caught fire!

It spread as swift as thought!

Lest the whole plain go up, Wulfston had to concentrate *now* on stopping that wildfire—and while he was doing so the riders were closing in, Traylo and Arlus growling and nipping at the horses' feet, barely escaping being pounded into the ground.

In this environment, Wulfston could not use fire, his most effective device to stop horses.

But he could buckle the knees of the one now approaching him, as if a net had entangled its feet. It went down, dumping its rider in a heap, and Wulfston concentrated for a moment on sending the man deep into unconsciousness.

There were still eight riders.

He sent another slumping into Adept sleep, but the method was too slow. He could not stop the other seven before they netted him.

His own knees buckled as a wave of dizziness swept over him—there were minor Adepts among them, joining their powers against him! If they could make him waste enough energy—

He shook off their attempt, and darted between two horses, pushing the animals apart with sheer Adept strength. That was working directly against nature, not an act he could perform very often, especially when he was not in peak condition.

But how could he work *with* nature here? Fire was too dangerous, and the little animals of the plain too small to do any good.

Then he remembered—down there by the lake—he

concentrated, creating a fear, a need to move, to run in this direction—

As his mind went off in search of his weapon, the riders circled him again, nets spread—

Again the attack on his mind—he fought it—flailed at the descending net—

He was tangled!

Adept power tore through the wiry strands, but not without cost. Wulfston could feel his powers weakening as he regained his feet, tossing the shreds of the net from him.

The horsemen turned, surrounding him again.

A pounding louder than the horses' hoofs shook the plain.

The herd of water buffalo, drawn by Wulfston's message, stampeded toward the riders!

Their horses screamed, bucked, and galloped off to save their own lives, carrying their riders along, like it or not.

Wulfston called Traylo and Arlus, gathered them close against him and held the terrified pups still while he concentrated on separating the mindless stampede around them. Choking dust rose, hoofs pounding within a hand's span on either side, but Adept concentration gave them a tiny island of safety as the herd thundered past, driving Wulfston's would-be captors eastward toward the jungle.

When the herd was gone, he remained, still holding the whimpering dogs, deliberately guiding the buffalo to force the riders to the edge of the jungle, miles away. They would come back, he knew—and he wanted to be far away before they did.

Finaly, Wulfston released his concentration, and calmed the two pups. He looked around at the flattened grass, the settling dust, and knew a moment's triumph. He was alive—he had survived in this strange land, won against enemies who knew the territory.

He turned back toward the lake . . . and saw the smashed, dead body of the rider he had sent to sleep. In his concentration on saving himself, he had forgotten the completely helpless man.

As he stared at the mangled body, though, he remembered that even though these men had obviously had orders to take him without killing him, they would have carried him off to face death . . . or worse.

It would be best if Sukuru or Z'nelia—or both—thought him dead.

Distasteful though the work was, he stripped the bloody clothing off the corpse, took off his loincloth, smeared it with the man's blood, and put it on the body. The man's face was smashed beyond recognition—and the scavengers of the plain would begin their work before the riders could get back here. Let them think two men had died here, and the jackals had carried off one of the bodies entirely.

Naked, Wulfston carried the dead man's clothes back to the lake and washed them. The fresh blood came out easily in the cold water, and there were only a few tears in the cloth.

This time he used his powers to dry the material, and studied the clothes: a tan tunic with a braided belt, and a faded yellow hooded cloak. Nondescript, and similar to what the other riders had worn. Plain leather sandals also had no identifying marks that Wulfston could see.

There were also a wristband with a pattern burned into it, and a talisman of some sort on a leather thong. These he buried deep in the sand, then put on the dead man's clothes, uncomfortable at the thought, but knowing no other way to blend in than to dress like someone who lived here. Surely he would be less conspicuous this way than stark naked!

As if to confirm that he was doing the right thing, when Wulfston turned to look for Traylo and Arlus he saw a horse approaching the lake—the dead man's horse that had run off before the stampede, now over its terror and seeking water.

The horse put Wulfston on equal terms with his pursuers.

Furthermore, there was a leather water bag attached to the saddle. He emptied out the warm dregs and refilled it with fresh, cool water from the lake.

There were saddlebags, with the same design burned into them that he had seen on the man's wristband. They would have to be buried, too, but first he searched them, and found bread and cheese, an apple—and a knife!

He devoured the food, stuck the knife through his belt, and continued the search. A pouch of coins! Coppers only, but at least a means of buying more food. There was also a small packet containing one bone and one metal needle and a folded paper of salt, which he put in the coin purse and suspended from his belt.

There was only one more item, a well-worn wooden plaque whose design appeared to be lettering rather than decoration. He wondered if Aradia could have read the language—she had shared their father's love of books gathered from all over the world.

But the plaque might be identified, so it was buried with the saddlebags. Wulfston mounted the horse, called to the dogs, and set out for that wagon trail to the south, counting on the footprints of the animals who would come to drink at the lake during the night to obscure his trail along the shoreline.

That night he slept in one of the buildings he had seen from the eagle's point of view. They turned out to be a deserted village, but gave Wulfston shelter for himself and the horse and dogs.

At dawn he set out along the wagon track again, spending the long hours practicing his rapport with Traylo and Arlus, or with other animals. He saw no people all day, just herds of wild animals. No wagons had been on this trail for days, for new grass was struggling to grow even in the ruts.

Its struggle was not entirely successful, though, for there had obviously been no rain recently—even the deepest ruts were dry. There were no rain clouds in sight; the sun beat yellow on the yellow plain, and Wulfston was grateful for the lightweight cloak with its hood to protect his head.

He sensed no pursuit. He hoped his ruse had worked, and his enemies thought him dead. It would give him time to find out what had happened to his friends.

Again he hunted, and shared fresh meat with the dogs, while the horse cropped the dry grass. When there was no watering hole, he figured out the use of a sort of leather bowl dangling from the bridle—he could pour some water from the water bag to share with the horse. Traylo and Arlus drank from it, too.

By noon of the second day on the deserted trail they were out of water.

The character of the land had changed: although the ubiquitous grass grew here now, the land was furrowed, as if it had been plowed and a crop grown at some time in the past year. In this part of the world, it appeared that crops would be grown in the rainy season, and the fields left fallow during this dry time of year.

Plowed fields had to mean people close by.

Wulfston wasn't sure he was ready to meet anyone, yet he needed to trade coins for fruit and vegetables. And he had to find out where his friends were.

He also had to learn to Read people, not just animals.

So he stuck to the wagon track, getting more tired and thirsty with every step, wondering where the nearest settlement was.

Instead of a village he saw in the distance a cluster of green trees. That meant water! The dogs smelled it and ran eagerly ahead, and the tired horse picked up his pace when Wulfston urged him.

On closer approach, he saw a stone well, and off to one side a cluster of houses. Only one person was to be seen; a young woman who had just filled a jug at the well, and was walking in the direction of the houses.

Wulfston hoped she would keep going, as he wanted to

renew his water supply and be ready to retreat if he ran
into trouble. The girl glanced at him, but continued on
her way—probably taught not to talk to strangers. He
could see why. In his lands she would be safe enough
today, but there had been a time when such a pretty
young girl would not have dared stray so far from home
alone.

Wulfston's attention turned from the girl to the well.
He hadn't known how thirsty he was until he was in sight
and smell of water!

He swung down off his horse, strode to the well, and
dropped the bucket into the water below. The splash was
the most welcome sound he had heard all day. He licked
dry lips as he added Adept strength to cranking up the
winch, grabbed the bucket, raised it to his lips, spilling
water on himself as—

Something stung him in the neck.

He let go the bucket with one hand to slap at it, but his
hand did not connect. It fell to his side limply, the fingers
of the other hand releasing the bucket, which fell back
into the well.

Wulfston's knees gave way as he tried to turn in the
direction from which had come—

—a dart.

The girl stood not ten paces away, a blowgun in her hand.

Wulfston tried to speak, but he was falling, out of control of his body.

He reached instinctively for his Adept powers to drive
the poison from his blood, but it was as if he had used up
every bit of his energy! He could do nothing—nothing—
except stare up helplessly at the girl who bent over him.

Traylo and Arlus snarled at the girl as she reached to touch
him, but she smiled at the dogs, and in moments they were
fawning on her, letting her scratch them behind the ears.

Paralyzed, bereft of his powers, Wulfston could do nothing but stare, the greatest fear he had ever felt in his life
tearing at his guts.

Chapter Four

*V*oices drifting in the darkness.

Two women. What are they saying?

Wulfston's mind made snatches at the words buzzing around in his head, but could only make sense of a few.

Trader's Common? No. The other language, taught by—

What was her name? Chaika? Eyes. Only her eyes can be seen. Eyes so much like . . . whose?

WHAT'S WRONG WITH ME?

For a moment Wulfston's mind was startled into coherence, but he could not maintain it. Confusion returned.

He tried to open his eyes, but the lids stubbornly refused to move.

Drugged. Drug on that . . . dart. Must call up healing . . .

But his powers would not obey him. No matter how he tried, he could not make the healing fire flow through his blood.

My powers . . . gone?

Fear pushed some of the cobwebs from his brain. He was in acute discomfort, his tongue and throat raw and swollen.

He remembered stopping at the well, thirsty. That's where he had been captured!

His flailing mind seized that thought. *I'm a prisoner, and they've drugged me so I can't use my powers to escape.*

A mixture of anger and fear charged his blood, helping

to bring him to his senses. He lay in a soft bed. The air was warm and dry, had a "morning" smell. Aching joints announced themselves, but his attempts to stop the pain met with failure.

No powers.

He forced himself to calm his mind. For the moment, rational thought was his only weapon.

My Adept powers will return, he told himself firmly. *Reading doesn't require energy, so perhaps—*

But his attempt to reach out with his mind, to summon Traylo and Arlus, also failed. He could not even sense them, nor any animal life.

Reading might not require strength, but illness and injury curtailed it severely. The drug on that dart had made him so ill that he could not even open his eyes.

The pain in his throat flared. He gave an involuntary moan. The women stopped talking. Wulfston heard them approach the bed. Gentle fingers pushed open his eyelids, and his eyes slowly focused on two concerned faces. They propped him up against some cushions, and one of them brought the mouth of a small clay bottle to his lips.

The liquid that poured over his parched tongue had a sour taste, but it cooled the fire in his throat and eased the queasiness in his stomach. The woman let him have only a little at a time, so he would not choke.

His thirst satisfied, Wulfston managed a weak smile in lieu of thanks. Both women smiled in return. Discovering that his tongue would move, Wulfston tried to say "thank you" in Trader's Common. One of the women closed her eyes, and for a moment he "heard" the distant echo of a woman's voice in his head, speaking foreign words.

He was Reading her thoughts!

Despite his situation, this long-dreamed-of moment buoyed his spirits. He wanted to laugh and shout for joy, but had no strength. *At last I'm a Reader! A very weak one, apparently, but that will change as soon as I get some training from—*

Lenardo.

The rescue mission.

His elation disappeared as he remembered why he was here.

He heard—no, Read—the woman's thought again, the same words repeated; she was sending a message to someone. Soon another female voice echoed in his mind. He got the impression that she was a short distance away.

He could not understand the words, but sensed orders being given concerning his welfare—and something else. As the message continued, the young Reader's facial expression changed several times; mild surprise . . . consternation . . . wry amusement.

What's being said about me? he wondered, then tried to project the question to the Reader beside his bed.

Either she couldn't understand or was ignoring him. She spoke rapidly to her companion, who stared at Wulfston with the same series of reactions.

The atmosphere suddenly chilled. Wulfston discerned that the mysterious message had changed his status from patient to prisoner.

Or to someone's property.

The irony did not escape him.

Not so many years ago he had captured a badly injured Lenardo and taken him to Aradia, who had healed him but claimed the Aventine Reader as her property. At the time, Wulfston had felt as she did: whatever an Adept could hold was his to keep by right of nature.

Now someone wants to keep a Lord Adept, he thought. *And in my present condition, there's not a thing I can do about it!*

Again the women propped him up to a sitting position, but the clay bottle they brought him this time smelled like wine. It had a bitter taste. Wulfston tried to avoid swallowing it, but one of the women stroked his throat, forcing the swallow reflex. Instantly, his feeble attempts at resistance dissolved, and the women lowered him back to the cushions.

No amount of drugs will make me anyone's property, he thought defiantly as drowsiness overcame him. *I will regain my powers and rescue Lenardo . . . if I have to fight all of Africa to do it!*

He dreamed he was back on the grass plains again, trying to evade capture. Herds of wild beasts scattered at his approach. A dozen paces ahead of him, a giant eagle stood on the ground as though waiting to carry him away from his pursuers. But before he could touch it, the great wings spread and it was instantly aloft.

Wulfston was surrounded by a dozen women in long dresses and veils. They approached as though sure he could not escape. He tried to use Adept force to drive them back, but found himself powerless, stripped of all his talents!

The women formed a tight circle around him, each one raising a long dagger. He leaped for the throat of the woman immediately in front of him, feeling more like a beast than a rational man as he tried to strangle the life out of her. Her knife thrusts somehow missed him as they struggled . . . struggled . . . struggled until her neck snapped and her veil fell off—

Revealing the face of his sister Aradia!

Wulfston was shaken awake. Groggily he stared at the two very large men who dared thus handle a Lord Adept, but neither his powers nor his body would obey his will. He remembered where he was.

Or did he?

He was in the same room where he had awakened before, but as the two men helped him to sit on the edge of the bed his feet touched stone, not earth. The walls were also stone. This could not be one of the wooden huts he had seen near the well where he was captured!

The men determinedly urged him toward a wooden
tub. As he gathered that they wanted him to bathe, he
realized that his clothes had been removed while he slept.
The water was warm, and scented with spices. As he sank
into it, the warmth eased the paralysis out of his muscles.

Still silent, the men handed him soap and a sponge,
then stood back and waited. Wulfston studied them as he
washed away the sweat of illness and bad dreams.

His guards—or whatever their function—were night-
black giants with no trace of humor in their faces. Like the
horsemen who had pursued him, they wore tan tunics,
but these garments were emblazoned with a black lion's
head in the center of the chest. Wulfston gathered that it
was the mark of some elite group—palace guards?

Palace?

That was it—the place felt like his own castle. He
glanced at the room's only window, and saw the branches
of strange trees at eye level. They were above the ground
floor. The rosy glow of sunset filtered through the trees.

His attention went back to the guards, who stood grimly
waiting for him to finish his bath. Why so grim? They
were not mistreating him, but he suspected they resented
their orders to nursemaid him. *Whose* orders?

Why had whoever was in charge decided he needed
two strong men as guards? He was certainly no threat in
his present condition. The guards had shaken him awake,
even though the only safe way to waken a powerful Adept
was with a light finger touch on the forehead. So they
were sure his powers would not manifest, as he verified
when he found that he could not even strengthen his
limbs with Adept energy.

Could it mean that his Reading powers were growing?
Dominating his Adept talents?

No, he realized as soon as he tried them, *whatever
small Reading talents I had have deserted me, too*. He
could not even Read the surface emotions of the two men.

"Where am I?" he asked them, first in Trader's Common, then in Zionae. Both attempts earned him only stares, and an apologetic shrug from one of the men.

The bathwater was cooling, so he turned his efforts to scrubbing himself clean. The brown soap they had given him was much coarser than even the cheapest at home, and he wondered what other differences he would find. Chulaika had hinted—

Chulaika. Chaiku. Zanos. Astra. Huber.

Are they still alive? he wondered on a stab of guilt at having been completely consumed with his own survival. *And where are they?*

While Wulfston toweled himself dry with a huge sheet of sheer, soft cotton, one of the guards laid out clothes for him. They were impressive, but nothing like what he was accustomed to: a black loincloth of soft, satiny material; a gold satin tunic with matching trousers that tie-cinched at the waist; and a pair of black leather sandals.

He was handed a large wooden comb resembling a flat, oversized fork, and discovered that it was a better instrument for controlling his hair and beard than the combs and brushes he struggled with at home. As he stood before a small, circular mirror affixed to one of the walls, the image that stared back at him began to resemble his old self. His beard needed trimming, but he still looked reasonably neat, and felt much better about facing . . . what?

Casually, he tried to slip the comb into his tunic—it could make quite an effective weapon—but one of the guards snatched it out of his hand the moment he finished grooming his beard.

"Well? What now?" he asked rhetorically.

One of them opened the door. Wulfston followed him out, and the other guard brought up the rear.

Elaborate candleholders lined the corridor. Wulfston noted that the stone walls appeared new—not much older than the walls of Castle Blackwolf, completed two years before.

Near the stairs that appeared to be their destination, Wulfston stopped to look out a window. The second guard nudged him, but Wulfston held his ground to get a view of the outside of the castle. Stretching away before him were the dark outlines of a small community under a dusky sky. Lights were coming to life in structures resembling the buildings of Zendi. This was a city, not a primitive village.

Just below him, workers were constructing a stone wall, hauling stone and mortar up wooden scaffolding to a height perhaps two stories above the ground. The first story had been completed around the castle for as far as he could see in either direction. The workers passed tools and materials with the precise, efficient movements of people who had labored together for a long time.

His patience at an end, the second guard took Wulfston's arm and urged him down the stairs. Still unaccustomed to such treatment, Wulfston glared at him—and noted a glimmer of fear in his eyes. So. The guards knew he had powers . . . and that the drugs they had given him would not deprive him of them forever.

Feeling relief from a fear he had been unable to acknowledge, Wulfston began considering how he might escape as he turned and continued down the stairs.

At the bottom they entered a wide, high-ceilinged foyer. To his left were the massive iron doors of the castle's main entrance, closed and barred. To his right were an impressive pair of teakwood doors, also closed, each with the face of a roaring lion carved in its center.

The two guards now flanked him, pausing for a moment before the doors. Wulfston squared his shoulders and took a deep calming breath as they pushed open the doors and ushered him into—

—a gallery of a hundred silent, staring people.

Two stone tiers, each higher than a man was tall, curved around the huge room in a semicircle. Seated on each level were perhaps a dozen ebony-skinned men and women in high-backed thronelike chairs.

Each was dressed in elaborately embroidered finery, some in robes similar to Aventine fashion, others in gowns or caftans such as he associated with Africa. About each person's neck was a talisman on a gold chain. All had the bearing of rulers.

Each chair was flanked by two people standing, some hulking bodyguards, some more like his own retainers at home. All were impressively attired, as were the two dozen or so men and women standing on the floor level, against the curved wall directly ahead of him.

Emotion charged the air. People stared, pulling back in their seats as Wulfston and the two guards strode into the brightly lit chamber. It felt for one moment as if this vast assembly of strangers recognized him—with fear.

The mood was dispersed by the sudden yapping of dogs. Wulfston was unreasonably pleased to see Traylo and Arlus, even though they were leashed and restrained by two men flanking a young woman at the center of the lower tier.

Wulfston recognized her: the girl with the blowgun at the well!

His captor.

But now she was resplendent in a gold gown, her hair elaborately upswept—no village maiden this, but a woman of consequence.

When the guards stopped, so did Wulfston. His mind was on that girl/woman of catlike beauty, green-eyed and serene. She smiled enigmatically as she reached one hand to the head of each pup. Their barking ceased at once, and they sat like well-trained house pets.

Wulfston felt as subdued as the dogs. He wanted to bide his time, see what was asked of him, store up information, but he dared not appear passive and compliant.

A throat cleared, pulling his gaze upward to a middle-aged woman on the upper tier, directly above the woman in gold. She had the same catlike air, but in the older woman it was more like that of a lioness staring at her dinner. Her resemblance to the younger woman was unmistakable.

"Lord Wulfston of the Savage Empire," she said coldly, "I am Ashuru, Queen of the Karili Nation." Her voice was soft, but it resounded clearly off the chamber walls. She spoke Trader's Common with an accent much different from Sukuru's or Chulaika's. "We would know why you have invaded our lands."

"Invaded!" Wulfston's first impulse was to defend himself, but the peculiar feeling that these strangers knew him when he knew nothing of them kept him from going beyond the single word of disbelief.

He remembered Nerius teaching him, "When powerful Adepts first meet, each seeks to impress, dominate, or intimidate—or to make the other appear to brag or bluster. Whether you sit on your own throne, or stand before another's, you must gain the advantage and maintain it."

The queen leaned forward. "Well?" she prompted.

My advantage, thought Wulfston. *She displays impatience before her peers.*

He countered with a contemptuous glance at the guards on either side of him.

Ashuru recognized that she had given him the upper hand, for he distinctly heard a low, angry sound come from her throat. She dismissed the two guards with a wave of her hand. They bowed and retreated.

"Now," said the queen, "explain your presence in our lands."

Excellent—he was now a presence rather than an invasion.

"Explain why," he countered, "when I was shipwrecked on your shores, I was three times attacked when all I sought was to survive."

"You entered Karili lands, wearing Karili clothing from one of our people you murdered," Ashuru replied.

"*Entered* your lands thus attired," Wulfston noted. "Then the man whose clothing I appropriated came *out* of your lands to attack me. I have done nothing to provoke your people, yet ever since I arrived in Africa my life has been in peril. Finally you," he said, directing his gaze to the young woman in gold, "shot me down as I sought to quench my thirst. In my land, no stranger goes thirsty when there is water available."

"You killed Gorimu, the son of one of our allies," a new voice suddenly spoke up. It belonged to the young man standing beside the woman in gold. He bore a strong resemblance to her, but was a bit younger. "In recompense, my sister Tadisha had to risk her life to capture you."

No wonder Ashuru hates me, Wulfston realized. *A mother whose child has been endangered.*

"Queen Ashuru, Princess Tadisha, and Prince . . . ?"

"Kamas," the boy supplied.

Wulfston continued, "I assume that Gorimu was one of the men who attacked me in the grasslands. Another party tried to kill me on the beach. My ship was destroyed without so much as a warning, before I could even land—and *I* am the one accused of wrongdoing? Africans came to my land, and stole my brother Lenardo. They forced me to come to Africa against my will. Help me find Lenardo. I will take him home with me, and never set foot in Africa again."

He felt Tadisha's eyes on him, although he kept his gaze fixed on Ashuru. Beside the queen, a very old man stood peering at Wulfston, giving him the sense that his every word was being absorbed and examined, all nuances behind it unveiled. A Master Reader, he suspected, or the African equivalent. Someone capable of determining whether he spoke the truth, as long as he did not brace his Adept powers.

The old man leaned forward and asked, "You have a brother? Is he not then a powerful Mover like yourself?"

Wulfston looked deliberately at the man, who appeared to be of Master Clement's age. His face was wrinkled so that his eyes sank deep into his skull, bright coals glowing amid a dying fire. There was somehing else in those eyes, something very different from Master Clement's calm benevolence, yet Wulfston sensed that this man knew him, and would reveal the truth of what he said.

From years of experience with Readers, Wulfston knew how to drop his mental defenses so that there could be no question of his honesty. Staring the old man in the eye, he did so now, for he had nothing to hide. "Lenardo is my sister's husband, a Master Reader."

"A sister," the old Reader murmured significantly. Wulfston was annoyed; he didn't want to explain that Aradia had not come because she was pregnant. He wanted to get on with the search for Lenardo. Instead of asking the expected question, though, the old man stared trancelike at nothing for a moment, then said, "Your sister, but not by blood."

Wulfston realized he must have seen the image of Aradia in his mind, which would certainly show anyone they were not blood-related. To forestall any further questions, he looked back to the queen and repeated, "Queen Ashuru, I do not want to be here. Will you help me find Lenardo, so that I may leave your lands?"

Before the queen could reply, her daughter said, "He did not ride into the village as an attacker, Mother. He appeared to be just what he said, a thirsty traveler seeking water. With his powers, he could have easily taken those poor people if he had wanted them."

"Barak?" questioned Ashuru, looking toward the aged Reader.

"Your daughter discerns the truth," he replied. "Lord Wulfston did not come to invade Africa."

Ashuru did not seem particularly pleased to have Wulfston declared innocent, but he was relieved, saying, "Thank you, Master Reader."

The old face crinkled in a sad smile. "I am not a Seer—Reader, as you call such in your lands. I am a Grioka."

"Grioka?"

'Storyteller," Ashuru explained, "although that is not an adequate description of Barak's function. My daughter and I are Seers, but we expected you to approach us shielded with your Mover's powers, preventing us from Seeing the truth of your words. Your history cannot be hidden from a Grioka."

"I don't understand," Wulfston said. Even Lenardo could not Read an Adept braced to use his powers.

"I cannot See your thoughts," Barak explained. "When I am in your presence, however, I know your history. Lord of the Black Wolf, I know who you are."

Only later was Wulfston to realize the significance of Barak's words. At the moment his concern was to find out where Lenardo was. In the days he had been drugged and helpless, Sukuru could have taken the Reader almost anywhere. "Then you know that I came to Africa against my will. Does anyone here know where Sukuru is? He is the one who stole Lenardo. He had heard an exaggerated story about my Adept prowess—that I had defeated Drakonius single-handed. Perhaps he heard the tale from you, Barak?"

Barak studied him. "I have told this story," he admitted. "The one from whom I learned it believed it. But Sukuru?" The Grioka frowned. "I do not know any Sukuru. And I would surely remember any man for whom I told such a rare tale."

"Whether he was the one who called for the telling, I don't know," said Wulfston, "but the story brought him to me. When I would not leave my lands to fight in a cause I knew nothing of, he kidnapped Lenardo to force me to follow him to Africa. I have already lost many days. I don't know if Sukuru still has Lenardo. Z'Nelia attacked my ship; how do I know she did not also destroy his? He professed to be her enemy."

"Z'Nelia?" Ashuru scoffed. "Lord Wulfston, Z'Nelia is queen of a small country on the other side of Africa. She doesn't have to power to wreck a ship on the west coast!"

Wulfston was about to protest, when he saw the expression on Barak's face. The man was at war with himself. In the silence left by Wulfston's lack of reply, the Grioka finally said, "Queen Ashuru, it is true. Z'Nelia *does* have such power."

The whisper of a drawn breath swept through the assembly, and suddenly everyone was staring at Barak. "Why," asked Ashuru, "have you never told us this?"

"The time was not fulfilled, until today," the Grioka replied.

"And so we have had only rumors!" the queen said angrily. "Four years ago the Savishnon warriors were stopped in Z'Nelia's lands . . . and no one knew how. All that remains where the battle took place are the Dead Lands, which no Seer may investigate, for to seek to See into them is to die!"

Wulfston had deliberately kept himself open to Reading all this time, and now even his limited powers were overwhelmed with Ashuru's fury. Thank the gods it was directed at Barak, and not at him! The queen continued, "My own teacher died, his spirit trapped in the Dead Lands, attempting to discover what had happened at Johara—and all the time, Barak, *you knew?*"

Barak said, "This tale I intended never to tell."

The members of the Assembly stirred again, and Ashuru voiced their rage. "We face the Savishnon, and possibly Z'Nelia's powers as well, and you would have left us in ignorance?"

But it was to Wulfston Barak spoke. "Shangonu willed

that I repeat the tale that is responsible for your presence here, Lord of the Black Wolf. I fear you will have to fight Z'Nelia, whether you wish it or no. If I tell now of Z'Nelia's defeat of the Savishnon, and the making of the Dead Lands, perhaps you will learn something that will allow you to survive."

The Assembly fell silent, and even Ashuru's mental fury abated as all waited for the Grioka to begin.

Barak's words were stock phrases of bards the world around, but as Wulfston listened, the Assembly faded away, and they were at the city of Johara, four years earlier. It was like nothing he had ever experienced listening to a bard; he knew things as if he had lived in Africa all his life, felt the apprehension of the people of Johara. . . .

Hordes of desert warriors swept down from the north, looting and burning and killing. In the name of their god, Savishna, they slaughtered all who opposed them. Their bloody trail spanned half the continent, but narrowed sharply at Johara, the richest and most beautiful city in Africa.

The six armies of Savishna surrounded the city's fortified walls while the commanders waited to see what futile ransom the royal family would offer. They failed to reckon with the powers and determination of Queen Z'Nelia.

Z'Nelia was not in Johara, although her Seers wove visions of deception to make the Savishnon Seers perceive her there. Two days before the armies arrived, Z'Nelia and her family had traveled to Mount Manjuro, to use their powers to waken the sleeping fire demon.

Only the queen returned from that perilous journey, her mount dropping with exhaustion as she arrived within the gates. "Tell our enemies," she instructed the Seers whose vigil had protected her city, "that here Savishna will meet his match."

As the message was delivered, Mount Manjuro thundered with renewed life.

When the Savishnon did not flee as she had hoped, Z'Nelia stood upon the parapets and summoned the fire demon. The sky grew dark. The mountain unleashed a river of death.

Liquid fire poured onto the plains surrounding Johara, burning everything in its path. The Savishnon had no time to flee; thousands of warriors were consumed in minutes. The few survivors fled, their dreams of conquest shattered.

Savishna sought revenge.

Strength already depleted from the steady use of her powers, Z'Nelia now fought to save her own people from the force she had unleashed. The river of fire lapped at the walls of Johara.

Other Movers supported her efforts, but fell, one by one, their powers exhausted. Z'Nelia stood alone, diverting the river of fire around her city, protecting her people to the last of her strength.

When finally the burning river began to harden into rock, it surrounded the entire city, but Johara itself remained an island in the frozen flow. Z'Nelia had saved her people.

The cost was all her strength. She dropped where she had stood, and as she lay helpless, a Savishnon spy who had infiltrated the city struck her with a knife!

He was killed at once by the mob, but it appeared he had accomplished his revenge. There were no healers for Z'Nelia. Every Mover in Johara lay unconscious, powers exhausted from trying to control the fire demon.

Seers rushed to Z'Nelia's aid, stanching the blood flowing from her wound, but until the next day no one with healing powers could help her . . . nor could the Seers reach her wandering spirit.

From the full moon to the third quarter, the healers of Shangonu's temple kept Z'Nelia's heart beating. Seers searched the planes of existence for her spirit—and their own spirits failed to return.

When the scattered Savishnon spread to other lands, bringing incoherent tales of what had happened at Johara, other Seers left their bodies to find out the truth—and lost themselves in turn. Hence the legend that to attempt to See into the Dead Lands—the lands ravaged by the fire demon—was to die.

The tale ended. Wulfston blinked, astonished to be back in the Karili Assembly.

He gathered his wits, and stared at Barak. "But Z'Nelia is alive and well now," he said. "What happened?"

"I do not know. When the lava cooled I left Johara. Some say the queen's eventual return to life and health was not accomplished by the priests and priestesses, that Z'Nelia found her own way back from the home of the dead. And she returned with more power than any Mover ever dreamed of possessing."

"That is an interesting story," Ashuru put in, "but there are many things that it does not tell—such as what happened to the others who went to the volcano. Z'Nelia's family. Who were they? Why didn't they return to Johara with her?"

"The others were Z'Nelia's husband, their son, and Z'Nelia's sister," Barak said. "Some say the fire demon demanded their lives in sacrifice."

"And what do people say who know that a volcano is a natural object, and not a god or a demon?" Wulfston asked.

"They say nothing . . . as Queen Z'Nelia would have it."

Wulfston wondered, "Have you been in Z'Nelia's presence since the events you have just described?"

He saw and felt Barak's hesitation, but before the Grioka could answer, the doors of the Assembly chamber were flung violently open, banging resoundingly against the walls, then remaining in place as a newcomer strode into their midst.

It was a plump, round-faced young man in elaborate green robes, carrying a spear like a walking staff. The spearhead glittered, and it took Wulfston a few moments to realize that it was actually made of a huge, long-cut *diamond*.

Its owner could not be even twenty years old. He was slightly shorter than Wulfston, and had the same brown skin tone. Again that whisper of surprise went through the gathered rulers, as it had when they first saw Wulfston.

But it was Barak's reaction Wulfston noted. The Grioka shrank back for a moment, as if he feared the younger man, but then he straightened determinedly, staring defiantly.

The boy turned his attention to Ashuru. "Members of the Karili Assembly," he said with a gesture toward Wulfston, "why has this prisoner not been sent to me as I ordered?"

"Because, Prince Norgu," Ashuru replied with a slight stress on the title, "you have no right to order the Karili in anything. You have our respect as ruler of the Warimu, no more. If you care to join our Assembly—"

"I am *King* of the Warimu," the boy replied, his attempt at insulted dignity coming out as a pout. "My powers are greater than any of yours. However," he added, rescuing himself from acting completely the fool, "I have come to offer you my help. I will take this dangerous invader into my custody, for you have other, far more serious things to concern you. The Savishnon are gathering again to the north of the plain. You need my powers, Ashuru. You need my armies."

"The Savishnon were soundly defeated four years ago," the queen told him. "They remain in small bands, an annoyance, but not a threat to a united front such as we represent. If you fear them, Norgu, you are welcome to join with us for protection."

"You are the ones who need protection!" the boy fumed.

"All your great Seers have not warned you of the danger. See with me!"

It was as if the diamond head of his staff came alive with light—whirling colors that resolved into a view of the plain with its herds of animals, to the north of the huge lake. Apparently Norgu shared some of the talent of a Grioku.

Then they were traveling northward. The herds of beasts disappeared. Bands of horsemen appeared, growing more numerous as they converged on—

—a camp of thousands!

Around the shore of a small lake an army was gathered. They were making weapons—arrows, spears, throwing sticks like the ones Wulfston's attackers had used along the shore. Wagons brought whole trees from the strip of jungle separating the plain from the sea, and craftsmen built catapults, a certain sign that walled castles like Ashuru's were included in their plans.

The vision faded.

"Norgu," Ashuru said, "we thank you for this warning, and welcome you to our company."

"I rule—"

"Will you waste your strength in a contest of powers when our common enemy is readying to attack?" Ashuru demanded.

"The Savishnon will attack here first," said Norgu. "If I do not aid you—"

"If you do not aid us," Ashuru replied, "we may be able to stop them, and we may not. If they defeat our combined powers here, you will stand alone . . . in their path toward their avowed destruction of the city of Johara! Alone, Norgu, you will be squashed like a beetle beneath the foot of an elephant."

"No one squashes me! Remember how I dealt with the assassins of Matu? Only a year ago, three assassins caught my father by surprise and killed him while his powers were weakened with use. Like you, they thought me too young to be a danger to them. But they were wrong!" He raised the diamond-headed spear. "They had lost the element of surprise. After they had murdered my father they turned on me, but I easily deflected their pain and their thunderbolts! Summoning my powers, I picked up my father's fallen spear, and with all my Mover's strength flung it at them, piercing all three bodies at once! Thus did I revenge my father's death. Thus did I become King of the Warimu. And thus will I treat all who deny me the rights Shangonu has given me with my powers!"

With that, Norgu leveled the spear at Wulfston, the diamond tip pointed at his throat.

"Would you be a Grioka, Norgu?" Barak suddenly challenged. "Then you must speak only truth. Child, you would like to believe this story as you have just told it, but you have not succeeded in destroying the actuality of that terrible day. What truly occurred was tragic—a wound you have yet to heal."

Again Barak's storytelling powers took them all to a different time and place. This time the scene was a village outside the walls of a castle—Norgu's castle. It was a sunny day. Women gathered at the river that ran nearby, to gossip as they washed clothes. They looked healthy and prosperous, as did the children splashing in the stream.

Norgu, looking slightly younger and even chubbier than he did today, walked beside an older man—his father, Matu, Wulfston knew with everyone else. The older man carried the diamond-headed staff.

Matu was instructing his son; Wulfston was strongly reminded of the days when Nerius took him out into the villages, and taught him his duties to their people.

The lesson was familiar. "While it is true that your people must fear your power, they should fear only to disobey. Do not be capricious, Norgu, or they will hate you. Hate can overcome even the greatest fear . . . and then your people will turn on you. If they have not the courage to attack you, they will simply fail to defend you from your enemies. And enemies rise quickly against the ruler who does not have the support of his people."

"But we are great Movers, Father," Norgu protested. "We can protect ourselves from our enemies."

Matu shook his head. "It is no blessing that your powers have developed so early, my son. Already they nearly equal mine, but I have the wisdom of experience. I have friends with powers—friends, Norgu, not servants or reluctant allies. If I need help in teaching you that no man can stand alone against the world, I will have it."

They came into the marketplace, where people turned to smile and bow as their ruler and his son passed.

Beside the well at the center of the market was a canopied stand with two thronelike chairs. Matu and Norgu took their places, and people began coming forward one by one with their petitions.

Wulfston was impressed. This was the way he had been taught to rule, making himself available to his people at certain times and places where no one could be turned away.

There were differences, though. He liked the way Matu and Norgu came alone, no guards or servants, into the midst of their people. It was friendlier than making them come into the castle—more like Lenardo's habit of taking petitions in the forum at Zendi, although he was always amidst a retinue.

Most of the petitions were for healing. The two Movers were also Seers, able to locate broken bones, infections, growths inside people's bodies, and thus work as the best healers did at home. Matu did most of the healing, Norgu observing as a Seer, learning the techniques.

Wulfston was interested in the way Matu used the diamond-headed staff, touching its head to his patients as if his power flowed through it. He had never before seen an Adept use an instrument to focus his powers. Once

Matu handed it to Norgu, and had the boy heal a vicious infection inside a man's bowel that had him in agonizing pain.

As the strain and paleness left the man's face, he looked up at Norgu and whispered, "Shangonu bless you," and drifted off into healing sleep.

Matu put a hand on his son's shoulder, and Norgu smiled at him. Then he returned the staff, and Matu continued with his work.

Wulfston estimated that the work Matu had done by then would leave an average Lord Adept weary—not exhausted, but ready for a good meal and a night's sleep. If Matu went on, it would suggest that his powers were beyond the average for a ruler, more on the level of Wulfston's or Aradia's.

Soon, though, Matu stood. "At the quarter-moon," he said, "there will be another healing day. None left among you is in pain, or has any problem that will be worsened by waiting until then."

"Excellent king!"

It was a cry of despair. Matu looked up sharply, and he and Norgu Read a ragged group of strangers guiding a rickety wagon drawn by a half-starved donkey. A woman ran forward, her emotions a jumble of grief and terror. "Oh, King Matu, please! My husband!"

On the wagon a man lay moaning, burned so badly that he hardly appeared human.

The moment Matu Read his pain he gasped, then sent the man to sleep, saying, "Bring him here at once."

Two men in hooded robes shoved the wagon forward while a third lashed the exhausted donkey.

Matu touched the diamond-headed spear to the injured man's forehead, and concentrated. Norgu Read that the patient was close to death, and was stepping forward to add his strength to that of his father when he suddenly Read something from the anxious woman.

Yes, the man was her husband, and yes, she was terrified for his life, but she was desperately trying to hide other fears—of the three men who appeared to be helping her!

Norgu turned his Seeing powers on them, and found them blank, braced to use Movers' powers.

"Father!" he cried—too late!

The same flames they had used to burn the poor man—their safe passage into Matu's village—suddenly consumed Matu!

Norgu's father gasped as flames roared through his clothing, seared his hair—

Then the fire was out, and he turned to face his attackers. A lightning bolt shot from the diamond-headed spear, and one of the three fell dead.

Norgu turned one of the others into a tower of flame, but it was out almost as it had begun. This was a powerful Mover!

With hardly a glance at Norgu, he reached out toward the other surviving Mover as Norgu saw his father stagger. They had made him use up the last of his strength!

The two Movers joined hands, concentrated—

Norgu wrenched the diamond-headed-spear from his father's unsteady hands and pointed it at the two Movers. Power flowed through him, concentrated in the diamond head—

And the bolt of lightning missed its mark as his father's scream jarred his concentration!

He turned to be splattered in the blood of Matu's exploding body!

Norgu screamed in turn, grief and rage mingled in pure animal savagery.

Now the two Movers were concentrating on him, but he had the spear. With the tip he caught the energy directed at him, all his strength concentrated on controlling, redirecting—

With a savage howl, he flung the power back at the closest of the attackers. The man's body sprung gouts of blood, his dying scream a drowning gurgle.

Panting with exertion, Norgu faced the last attacker. He reached for his Mover's powers, and found little left. But surely that other Mover was also exhausted. Reason was slowly returning; all he had to do to kill the man was stop his heart. That didn't take much effort.

He pointed the spear, concentrated—

The Mover faltered, but recovered. He raised his hand. Norgu knew he would send flame or lightning, and wasn't sure whether he still had power to deflect it, But—

The target was clear.

With all his physical strength, Norgu flung the diamond-headed spear straight into the heart of his attacker!

For a moment there was silence. Norgu waited numbly, emotions frozen.

Then, once he was certain his legs would obey him, he walked over to the still-quivering body, put his foot on it, and drew out the bloody spear.

He turned to where his father had been, where there were now only gobbets of flesh and splatters of blood.

The woman cowered beside the wagon, whimpering.

Norgu pulled her to her feet. She was already spattered in Matu's blood, but his hand left its print in red on her sleeve. "Go," he told her. "Take your husband, who is even now healing at the cost of my father's life."

"Prince Norgu, they burned him! I had to do what they told me—"

"And I should kill you for it," he replied, transferring his bloody hand to her throat. The terror in her eyes was sweet. "But who better than you to carry my message? Matu is dead, but Norgu lives! Norgu lives and holds power; let others come against me only at their peril."

He turned, eyes raking over the silent villagers, who had witnessed the entire scene. "So much," he announced loudly, "for Matu's belief that his people would protect him! Let it be known that Norgu will protect himself—and not waste his powers on the likes of you!"

Again Wulfston experienced the disorientation of returning from the Grioka's vision to the present in the Karili Assembly chamber.

Norgu was glaring at Barak, but the Grioka seemed to have no more fear of him. So the young prince turned to Ashuru. "This tale still presents ample evidence of my powers—which have grown since that day. You need—"

"Norgu, *you* need a parent's teaching," said Ashuru. "We all feel for your terrible loss, but it is a loss to us, too, for Matu would have taught you to be a wise ruler as well as a powerful one. As it is, you are a fifteen-year-old boy with powers you do not know how to use properly."

Norgu is only fifteen! Wulfston thought in astonishment. *No wonder he acts childish: he is a child—an extremely dangerous one.*

Ashuru obviously knew that. She was trying again to persuade Norgu to join with the Karili Assembly against the Savishnon. "There may be none of us here with the powers you will have when you are fully mature," she ended, "but we have a wealth of experience, Norgu. Let us teach you as Matu would have, so that you will be a great king one day."

"I need none of your teaching about how to be weak! But you need my help against the Savishnon. Give me this prisoner—he gestured toward Wulfston once again—"and I will join my powers with yours."

"Lord Wulfston is not a prisoner!" Tadisha spoke up. "He has spoken truly to us before the Grioka, and opened his mind to our Seeing powers. No one in Africa has the right to hold him prisoner, Norgu."

"Does your daughter speak for you, Ashuru?" Norgu asked.

The Karili queen looked around the assembly, getting nods from every direction. "She speaks for us all."

"Then I speak for myself!" Norgu spat. "You can face the Savishnon without my help, but when this man brings on your destruction"—he pointed to Wulfston with his left hand, the one not holding the spear—"you can remember that I would have kept him away from you if you had let me!"

Wulfston hardly heard the last words Norgu spoke. He was staring at the boy's left hand. On it shone a gold ring in a familiar shape. He had to see it up close!

Norgu spun, cloak swirling dramatically, and stalked out of the Assembly chamber. Without a thought, Wulfston started after him.

"Lord Wulfston!" It was Tadisha's voice, but it held him only for one step. He had to see that ring, for it was as if Norgu had deliberately waved it before him.

"Prince Norgu!" he called.

The boy continued as if he hadn't heard.

Wulfston had to run to catch up to him, and they were out in the courtyard before he could pass the boy and stop, facing him, barring his path. "Prince Norgu, I believe you have knowledge concerning the man I am looking for: a Reader—Seer, you would call him—named Lenardo."

"This Lenardo," Norgu asked, cocking his head to one side, "he is a white man?"

"Yes," Wulfston replied, certain now that Norgu knew where he was. The boy had his left hand hidden beneath his cloak. Wulfston resisted the urge to grab for it and get a good look at that ring.

"Seer, I do not know," Norgu said, his manner now grave—but he was play-acting, putting on a false sympathy that grated on Wulfston's nerves as he continued. "A white man traveling with Zionae . . . Was he quite tall, with dark hair and beard?"

"Yes," Wulfston said tightly, afraid to let his mind hear the past tense.

"Then . . . you can but avenge his death."

"What? No—it couldn't be Lenardo!"

"The party of travelers," Norgu replied, "was attacked by other Zionae, under the orders of Z'Nelia. All—the people he traveled with and their attackers—were trespassing in my lands. It was reported to me. Too late, unfortunately. There was a battle of Movers, over before I arrived to drive them out. Everyone was killed, everyone on both sides."

"It couldn't be—"

"There was a woman with a small child in the party," said Norgu, and Wulfston's heart sank. Chulaika and Chaiku had obviously rejoined Sukuru. Shock created a buzzing in his ears as the plump young ruler went on, "The Zionae wore nothing that would identify them, but from the hand of the dead white man I took this."

Numbly, Wulfston put out his hand, and Norgu laid on his palm the gold ring. The intricate carving glinted, blurring as his eyes filled with tears—but not before he saw clearly the intertwined figures of wolf and dragon.

Chapter Five

Wulfston stared at the ring lying glittering on the palm of his hand. Lenardo dead? *No!*

Norgu swept on out the gate, to where his retinue awaited him.

Wulfston remained in the courtyard, stunned. He stumbled to the watering trough for the horses and sat on its edge, his legs weak with shock.

Traylo and Arlus came running from the castle, straight to Wulfston. Sensing his sorrow, they rubbed against him, whimpering. He slid the ring onto his right hand, then put one hand on the head of each dog. Their dumb compassion broke through the burning lump in his throat, and his tears fell.

His friend was dead. Not only would he miss him savagely, but how could he face Aradia? Aradia, who even now carried Lenardo's child?

He must go home at once. Aradia needed him more than ever. Lenardo's child would need her uncle to help raise and educate her in her father's stead. *And I'll do right by you, Lenardo,* he promised silently, twisting the ring on his finger.

Determination shoved his grief aside. He washed his face in the watering trough, and considered his situation. For the first time, neither the burly guards nor the two female Seers attended him.

But of course they could Read him whenever they wanted to. At least he could make it more difficult for them by

bracing to use Adept power. In fact, he realized, he had
been doing so instinctively ever since Norgu had told him
Lenardo was dead.

Now that the Karili had decided he was not their enemy, how much freedom did he have? He should be able
just to walk out of the castle, past the guards at the gate
. . . and into a land where he did not know the language,
customs, geography—

He had no money and no friends, but he had responsibilities. Zanos and Astra, Huber, any sailors who had
survived the shipwreck—he could not leave them stranded
in Africa. First he must find all who had survived. Then
they would have to barter their services for passage on a
ship home.

Distasteful as it was, the quickest way to earn passage
home was as mercenaries in the coming battle with the
Savishnon. The Karili had not persuaded Norgu to aid
them; they would probably welcome Wulfston's powers
joined with theirs.

Traylo and Arlus suddenly jumped to their feet. The
dogs turned as Wulfston did, and ran merrily wagging
their tails to greet the Princess Tadisha.

"Is the Assembly over so soon?" Wulfston asked, for he
had been about to go back and offer his help in return for
theirs in locating his friends.

"No. I asked Kamas to take my place," she replied.
"Lord Wulfston, I am sorry to hear of the death of your
friend."

So she had been spying with her Seeing powers—on
Wulfston or on Norgu? Was her sympathy real or feigned?
Cautiously, he opened to Reading, ready to reassert his
defenses at the first sign of betrayal.

He Read only genuine sympathy as Tadisha said, "You
called him your brother."

"We were closer than many of blood kin. And now,
because that fool Sukuru insisted on involving me in his
power play, Lenardo is dead."

At the renewal of his grief, Tadisha reached for his hands, saying, "It's not your fault! If we hadn't captured you. . . . I'm so sorry."

Her green eyes looked into his as she gripped his hands. Suddenly, painfully, the pressure increased. She gasped, "Norgu lied!"

"What?"

She dropped his left hand, and put both of hers around the ring on his right. "This ring—the man who wore it was alive when it was taken from him!"

He stared at her, too much afraid to suffer raw grief a second time to take hope from her words. "How do you know?"

"I have some power to See the history of objects. This ring is new, its history brief. There is much love in it, and no death."

"Maybe Lenardo just wasn't quite dead yet," Wulfston said. "Why would Norgu lie about—?"

//Tell Wulfston I am both alive and well. So he will believe you, tell him—//

//Lenardo? *Lenardo!*//

The "voice" in his head was so much like Lenardo's speaking voice that there could be no doubt.

//Wulfston? You can Read?!//

//Yes! Where are you?//

//Five days' journey from you. I must be very careful, for I am guarded by Seers. They think I've fallen asleep in my chair, out of boredom.//

//Are you out of body?//

//No. That I dare not attempt. The Seers were instructed by Norgu—in my presence—that if they found my body unoccupied at any time, they were to move it. I don't think you know—//

//I've been around Readers enough to have an idea,// Wulfston told him with a shudder.

Tadisha could no longer contain her astonishment. //Lord

Lenardo, you are Seeing from Norgu's castle—without
leaving your body?//

//Yes, Lady Tadisha—and I am trusting you not to betray me. Because I dared not leave my body, the only way
I had to find Wulfston was to follow Norgu.//

//But five days' journey—//

//Lenardo is the best Reader in the Savage Empire,//
Wulfston told Tadisha impatiently. //Lenardo, I've been a
prisoner here, but they've stopped drugging me. I think
my powers will be back to normal soon.//

//Norgu hasn't drugged me at all,// Lenardo told him.
//It took nearly three days free of Sukuru's potions before I
felt completely myself. I'm well, but so far I've found no
way to evade the Seers Norgu has surrounding me.//

//I'll come to you,// Wulfston offered.

//Not alone,// Lenardo warned. //Norgu has powers.//

//He's just a boy,// Wulfston protested. //I am a Lord
Adept at the full strength of my powers.//

//I do not know the strength of your powers,// Tadisha
put in, //but never has one so young as Norgu shown such
power in Africa. And his army has many Seers and Movers,
fully loyal to him—they will combine their powers against
you, Lord Wulfston, if you attack.//

//If Lenardo can't escape, and I can't go to his rescue,
then how am I to free him?//

//I have an idea,// said Tadisha. //Lord Wulfston, neither
you nor the Savishnon are the primary reason the Assembly gathered here. It was Norgu's demand that we capture
you for him—as if he ruled us all. The Karili fear what
Norgu may be in a few years. Now, while he is still young,
we must thwart his domination.//

//Trust her,// said Lenardo. //Tadisha is telling the truth.
I will contact you again tomorrow, but I dare not remain
in communication for long, lest the Seers guarding me
discover it.//

And Lenardo's presence was gone.

Tadisha still held Wulfston's hand. Now she gave it a

tug. "Come back to the Assembly. They are arguing about what we should do now that we have three enemies."

"Three?"

"The Savishnon first. We must complete our defenses," she said with a gesture at the newly heightened walls, "for there is now no doubt of their attack. When I left, Mother was proposing riding out to meet them, trying to keep their destruction clear of our towns and villages.

"Second, Z'Nelia . . . perhaps. Until recently she kept to herself. We thought that whatever powers she had were destroyed or weakened in the battle that produced the Dead Lands. Then, a few months ago, her armies took the lands to the west of hers, on the other side of Norgu's. Now we learn that she can control a volcano, or raise a storm from across the continent. If she attacked you, why should she not attack anyone else who appears to be a threat to her?"

"Why would she perceive the Karili as a threat?" Wulfston asked. "Sukuru forced me to come to Africa specifically to battle Z'Nelia, so I must appear a genuine menace."

"Especially now that she has Seen you," Tadisha agreed.

"What do you mean?"

"You are Zionae," replied the Karili princess.

"I don't know what tribe my ancestors came from," Wulfston said, "but yes, I see resemblances in the few Zionae I've either met or Read—Seen."

"So if you defeated Z'Nelia, her people would be more likely to accept your right to rule them than the right of a foreigner."

"I *am* a foreigner. I have my own lands to rule, far from here," Wulfston told her as he had told Sukuru. "I don't want the lands of the Zionae."

"Perhaps you have come to take possession of the Warimu."

"The Warimu? Norgu's people?"

"Norgu is not Warimu, nor was his father."

"More Zionae," Wulfston realized. "Well, that makes

sense. With Z'Nelia ruling the Zionae, or earlier if her
parents were as powerful as she is, any Zionae Adepts—
Movers—who wanted to rule would find it easier to conquer another tribe than fight someone like Z'Nelia. But
Princess Tadisha, I don't want Norgu's lands, either."

"He will think you do, just as everyone in the Assembly
does."

"Why?"

"Because you and Norgu are so obviously related."

"Just because we're both of Zionae ancestry?"

"Didn't you see it?" she asked in astonishment. "It goes
far beyond tribal characteristics. You and Norgu have a
strong family resemblance."

"I don't look anything like Norgu!" Wulfston protested,
recalling the flabby, overweight boy with round face and
unpleasantly pouting features. "Besides, Barak would have
known, if he knows everything about people when he
meets them."

"Barak knows of you only what has happened in your
lifetime, unless you tell him stories of your family."

"I see," said Wulfston. "And if I had such stories, and
believed them to be true—"

"—he would perceive them as true, as he did the story
he was told of your prowess."

"Then a Grioka may be wrong."

"About stories and songs, yes. Never about direct experience," Tadisha explained. "The gods give the Griokae
that gift, and the ability to make hearers experience what
they tell. In return, the gods give them the obligation of
recording our history, and passing it from one generation
to another.

"Griokae are very wise," she continued, "and highly
respected. If we Karili offended Barak by chiding him for
his mistake about you, he might refuse to tell stories of us.
He would not teach them to other Griokae. Eventually,
the memory of the Karili would be gone from the history
of Africa, as if we had never been."

Wulfston saw in Tadisha's green eyes how very important it was to her that her people be remembered. "What if," he suggested, "Barak would not tell the story of Z'Nelia's defeat of the Savishnon before today, because she offended him, and he did not want her victory remembered?"

Her expression told him much. "That is a Grioka's only weapon against so powerful a Mover, but it is a mighty weapon indeed."

"So," said Wulfston, "the history of a person is that important here—so much so that because I do not know the history of my family you try to create one, by seeing a resemblance to Norgu?"

"I'm not the only one who saw it. When you first entered the Assembly, and again later, when you and Norgu stood side by side. You could be his brother, Lord Wulfston. You are certainly an uncle or cousin in some degree."

"Impossible."

To Wulfston's annoyance, laughter twinkled in Tadisha's eyes. "Are you that vain, then? I agree; Norgu makes himself unattractive with his overindulgence in food and his sneers and pouting. But let him harden his body with work, and gain maturity and character in his face, and one day he might be as handsome as you are."

Wulfston did not like that topic of conversation, or Tadisha's attempt to turn it to a joke. "Never mind Norgu's appearance. Why did he lie to me about Lenardo?"

"A childish fit of anger when the Assembly would not bow to his will?" Tadisha suggested.

"From someone who has been ruling his own lands for a year?" Wulfston asked. "That may have been part of it, but he could not survive many impulsive acts, considering the enemies he has."

"Perhaps he hoped you would leave if you thought your friend beyond your help."

"No . . . put yourself in Norgu's place, Princess Tadisha. Did you notice his reaction as he relived his father's death? There was no grief! He almost . . . reveled in the bloodshed." He looked into her eyes, trying to open to her Reading so that she would know he spoke truly. "I have seen such cases in my own land, among young people who have lost their families in the violence of Adept warfare. Their minds cannot cope with such grief. Their emotions become twisted. Norgu is very dangerous. There is no predicting how someone like that will react."

She nodded. "He will see you as a threat, especially if he recognizes that you are of his family. He must think you have come to take his throne. While I can See that you would indeed go home this day if he reunited you with your brother, Norgu probably fears that the two of you together would turn on him."

"I suspect," Wulfston said slowly, "that he is even more manipulative than that. He wants me to think that Lenardo is dead so that I will take revenge on his supposed murderer. Revenge Norgu understands. Remember his pleasure in destroying his father's attackers? But someone sent those killers, and Norgu has not yet had revenge on that someone."

Tadisha's green eyes showed grim understanding. "We Karili are too close to Norgu. We see him as a spoiled child, but he has developed a dangerous cunning. He told you Z'Nelia killed Lenardo. He must think Z'Nelia sent the men who murdered Matu—and of course he could be right."

Tadisha paused abruptly, staring at him. "I just realized that you never— Lord Wulfston, I do not think I have ever met a man before—at least not a man of such powers— whose first thought would not be of revenge." She lowered her eyes, suddenly closed to Reading. "Wise men would then put the thought from their minds, knowing revenge only brings more revenge. But what kind of man does not even consider it?"

"One who has witnessed a lifetime of war, and wants no more of it," he replied. "If Lenardo were truly dead, how would it help his people or his wife and children for me to risk my life in revenge? Those who counsel war would say if I did not kill Z'Nelia she would decide that I was weak, and soon she would come to the Savage Empire to depose me. But how likely is that, when she has her own battles right here?"

"That is true," agreed Tadisha.

"If, however, I challenged her, provoked her, either she would kill me now, leaving my sister without my help, or if I succeeded in killing or otherwise defeating her, her heirs would then seek revenge on me, perpetuating an enmity I never wanted in the first place."

Tadisha asked, "Where you come from, do you stand alone in these ideas?"

"No. One ruler cannot end the cycle of revenge; other lords would simply kill him and continue warring, the history of the Savage Lands before this generation. Our alliance is a precarious thing, which must be nurtured for the future. Were Lenardo dead, my first duty would be to go home and help to preserve it. As it is, my first duty is to rescue my brother. Will your Assembly allow me to address them?"

"I think so. Come, then, and I will present your petition."

Wulfston was, indeed, allowed to present his offer to aid the Karili against the Savishnon, in return for their help, first in locating his missing friends and the *Night Queen* crew, and then in retrieving Lenardo from Norgu.

"How much help can you be to us?" challenged Kamas.

"If you had not drugged me," Wulfston replied, "I could demonstrate my powers. Let me explain it this way: undrugged and rested, I can do all that you saw Norgu's father do in the vision Barak provided—and more. I also have many years' experience at teaching people with minor powers to use them to best advantage . . . and to unite them to overcome someone of greater power. If all of you were to work together, as the Movers and Seers of

my homeland do, even a Mover of Z'Nelia's powers would
be helpless against you."

"Would you then set yourself up as our leader?" Ashuru
questioned in acid tones.

"Not at all, Queen Ashuru," he replied, wondering why
she was suddenly hostile again. "You are the leaders of
your people; they will not follow a stranger. Nor do I
know your terrain, your languages, your customs. As soon
as the threat to you is over, and I am reunited with my
brother and the people we are responsible for, I will leave
Africa."

Finally Wulfston was dismissed, while the Assembly
debated accepting his offer. One of the burly guards appeared again, but this time the man bowed, led Wulfston
up a different flight of steps than those to his room, and
left him in a kind of study or library, reminiscent of the
one Aradia had lost when Castle Nerius was destroyed.

He found books, scrolls, and even clay tablets with
writing that looked like pictures of birds and animals. A
little investigation turned up several in the Aventine language, and even a few in the savage dialects. Those,
however, could tell him nothing he did not already know,
while the rest he could not read. For once he wished he
had Aradia's talent for languages.

Impatiently, he sat down in a comfortable chair before a
large table. He wanted to Read what was going on in the
Assembly, but was certain Seers would be on guard for
such spying. He wished he had Lenardo's powers, to
reach out and tell his friend this would be a good time to
converse. Lenardo hadn't mentioned Zanos, Astra, or the
others, but surely his Reading powers could find them!

Thinking of Lenardo's powers, though, reminded him of
his own, as did his growing hunger. How much of that
drug had worked its way out of his blood by now?

He glanced at a candle on the table and casually willed
it to light. Nothing happened.

He frowned, wondering why his Reading seemed to be

progressing nicely, when he could not seem to use even the simplest Adept power. Probably the vegetarian diet Ashuru had kept him on since his capture. He certainly hoped they would provide him with meat now that he was no longer a prisoner!

He concentrated on the candle as he had as a small boy, just learning to use his powers. To his relief, the flame sputtered to life. He resisted the temptation to start moving furniture, but settled back in the chair and set his concentration to drawing healing fire into his blood, purging away the last of the drug. He could not produce the normal rapid flare of energy, but he could feel his healing powers working as he relaxed and let his body cure itself.

Finally the door opened, and Tadisha entered. Her face, and the fact that she was closed to Reading, told him her news was not good. Wulfston sat up, alert, as she took a chair opposite him at the table and said, "My mother does not trust you—and her voice influences the Assembly."

"They won't help me?"

The princess shook her head. "They don't trust you because you are of Norgu's family. Blood will tell."

"I don't accept that," Wulfston told her. "Blood makes me look as I do, and gives me my powers, but how a person thinks and acts is determined by circumstances, and by family. And family often has nothing to do with blood. Neither Norgu nor any of his family shaped my thinking, Princess Tadisha."

"So said Barak. He told of the people you call family, all of them white. None of them taught you to be a Seer," she added. "Lord Wulfston, I recognized that your Mover's powers were far superior to your Seer's, but Lord Lenardo was astonished that you could See at all."

"It's true," Wulfston admitted. "I was unable to access my Seeing ability until I came to Africa. It was as if the life of the great plain spoke to me, and I responded as if . . . I had come home."

"Blood will tell," insisted Tadisha. "Your ancestors came

from the plains. The Zionae lived there for many generations, until the Savishnon caused them to flee to the east.
Many tribes hunt there, but it is a dangerous hunt today,
for the Savishnon claim that territory, and massacre anyone they find trespassing."

"Tell me more about the Savishnon," said Wulfston.

"They come from the far north of Africa, and worship
the war god Savishna. They believe their god has instructed them to conquer the entire continent. A generation ago they swept southward, onto the great plain,"
Tadisha explained. "Soon they took over the northern
areas of the plains, driving the tribes who lived there into
exile.

"Five years ago they began a new offensive, with an
army so huge none could count it. When my father,
Kagele, was killed, my mother persuaded the leaders of
other tribes to join us against the attackers. The Assembly
was formed. The Savishnon did not expect unity from our
many small tribes. We drove them back beyond the
great lake.

"We knew, though, that they would be back. We built
this castle, and fortified it strongly. Leaders of the tribes
set up communications via Seers throughout all the lands
now united with the Karili, and granted my mother the
right to call them together in any emergency."

"But the attack never came," said Wulfston.

"How do you know?" Tadisha asked.

"I grew up in a castle that bore the scars of Adept
warfare. There are none here—everything is new, perfectly matched."

"You are right," said Tadisha. "A year after we repelled
the Savishnon, they regrouped and attacked Johara. You
saw today what happened there. For the past four years
no more than scattered remnants of the Savishnon have
been seen."

Wulfston asked, "Do the Savishnon wear headbands?

Symbols on their foreheads in beads? I thought I saw some at their camp."

"Yes, whenever they go into battle."

"Then it was Savishnon who attacked me on the beach."

Tadisha nodded. "That is what we have come to expect the Savishnon to be: a constant annoyance, but no longer a threat to our way of life. We had hoped to rid all Karili lands of them."

"And now they are back as a well-organized army."

"One surprise after another," the princess agreed. "You are as great a surprise, if not so certain a threat. How is it you know nothing of your African origins?"

That again. He might as well tell her the little he knew. "I was only three years old when my parents died. I remember my mother telling me stories, but not the stories themselves. My father—my adopted father, Nerius— told me everything he knew about my family, but he knew only their history once they reached the Aventine Empire. They were proud citizens, Aventine to the core— which, now that I think about it, makes me wonder what they left behind that they were happy to work their way out of slavery, and apparently never pined for their homeland."

"Perhaps," said Tadisha, "you will discover the answer here in Africa."

"Perhaps I will," he agreed. "Torio told me I would find 'where I first began.' "

"Torio?"

"A Reader with the gift of prophecy."

"Ah. My family has that gift also," said Tadisha. "Proph-ecies always come true—in one way or another."

"I know," Wulfston said. "Torio said my fate was entangled with Lenardo's, and here I am. But Tadisha, if the Karili won't help me, then I must try to rescue Lenardo alone."

"I think," she said, her green eyes reflecting the candle

flame, "there may be a way to persuade the Assembly,
although my mother will be angry if I suggest it. She says
aloud that she fears what your presence here may do to
the precarious state of affairs in Africa. Privately, however,
she is concerned that I have become too . . . impressed
with you. Your ideas," she amended hastily.

Wulfston could not help smiling. He was finding himself
equally impressed with the Karili princess. "There is a
way," he said, "that you need not risk your mother's
displeasure. I am willing to go before your best Seers, and
make no resistance to their powers. In my homeland, the
process is known as the Oath of Truth, taken before a
panel of Master Readers."

But when they approached Ashuru, she waved the idea
away. She was in consultation with Barak, and Wulfston
found the scrutiny of the old Grioka almost palpable as the
queen said, "I have little doubt of your motives, Lord
Wulfston—as far as they go today. What concerns me is
your effect on the history of my nation."

At that Tadisha squared her shoulders. "Then, Mother,
you know what we must do. What I must do. When the
fate of our people is in the balance—"

"It is too dangerous!" hissed Ashuru, with a scowl at
Wulfston.

"Princess Tadisha, what do you propose to do?" he
asked.

"Seek a Vision of the future," she replied.

"You can produce prophecies on demand?" he asked in
surprise. Lenardo's flashes of precognition came without
warning, as did Torio's verbal predictions. Neither man
could control the gift.

"It is a most exhausting procedure," said Tadisha, "and
does not always provide answers. However, with the
Savishnon preparing to attack, Norgu refusing to help us,
and your presence an unexpected factor, I must attempt
it." She looked at her mother as if defying her to produce
a reason not to.

And Ashuru did. "Tadisha, you would risk your life. Since the routing of the Savishnon at Johara, too many Seers who have left their bodies have never returned."

"Only those who sought to See into the Dead Lands," Tadisha protested.

"Not entirely," said Barak. "I have heard tales of those being lost who merely sought to See at a great distance. Things are being Hidden, even from the Sight. Let beware any who trespass, even unintentionally, into areas that are Guarded."

Ashuru stared at the Grioka. "Barak, am I correct that you were as surprised as the rest of us at the vision Norgu brought of the Savishnon gathering north of the great lake?"

"You are correct. No one had told of it in my presence before."

"Yet Seers of all tribes have kept watch on the movements of the Savishnon. Until now."

"If Savishnon Seers have ensnared other Seers trying to spy on them, how did Norgu do it?" Wulfston asked. "The way he uses his Mover's powers, he can't be much of a Seer."

"I think," Barak said reflectively, "that the Vision was not through Norgu. He Saw it through another Seer. Forgive me, it did not occur to me at the time to seek to know. When I am next in his presence, I will discover it."

"What else do you not know, Barak—or have you withheld from us?" Ashuru asked.

"I do not know the future," the Grioka replied with transcendent dignity.

The Karili queen stared at him. "Do you say I am wrong, Barak? Would you have Tadisha risk her life seeking this Vision?"

From sunken depths, Barak's eyes fixed on Wulfston. "Queen Ashuru, everything I know of Lord Wulfston agrees with the reassurances he gives. But a man may change his mind without breaking his word."

"Indeed," said Ashuru, her eyes flicking from Wulfston to Tadisha and back again.

"We must know whether to accept Lord Wulfston's offer," said Barak. "Queen Ashuru, you must surely realize that this man will not go home without his brother. If he must, he will go alone to his rescue. He could be captured and used by Norgu, Z'Nelia, or the Savishnon. He could simply fail in the rescue, and blame you for refusing to aid him. Or he could find other allies."

"There is no guarantee that a Ceremony of Vision will give us the answers we seek," said Ashuru, "but it *will* risk my daughter's life."

"We can minimize the risk," said Bark, "and at the same time increase our chances of obtaining knowledge. Tadisha has the power of Vision very strongly, but you also have it, Ashuru. Enter the Vision with her—and so will I. Possibly my powers will enable us to find out what we seek."

The queen nodded slowly, reluctantly. "Yes, we can at least provide an anchor for Tadisha's spirit, lessen the danger of her being lost. My daughter?"

"You know I am willing, Mother."

"I want to be there," said Wulfston.

"No," Ashuru replied. "You know nothing of our ways. You could distract Tadisha at a crucial moment."

"Barak." Wulfston looked straight into the old man's eyes. "I have worked with Readers hundreds of times, and never distracted them. As a matter of fact, I once participated in a circle of power that drew a Master Reader's mind back to his body when it had been wandering, lost, for days. Verify that I will not distract you."

A small smile curved the Grioka's lips. "How quickly you have learned to use me, Lord Wulfston. You know that if you demand it, I must tell Queen Ashuru that you speak the truth."

"It makes no difference," said Ashuru. "I do not want you there."

"I do."

Ashuru's head turned sharply as she stared at her daughter.

Tadisha continued, "Lord Wulfston is the subject of the Ceremony of Vision, and I am the Seeker. It is my decision."

Wulfston was fast learning the negative aspects of Reading; Ashuru made no attempt to conceal her cold fury, but she was trapped. "Very well, Tadisha. Now, we must prepare."

Wulfston did not know what the preparations were for the Seekers. The two women and Barak went off to the temple, while Kamas was called upon to be Wulfston's host for a hearty meal. Studying the heavily laden board, Wulfston asked, "When will the ceremony take place?"

"It will begin at midnight," Kamas replied.

"May I trust you, Kamas?"

The younger man studied him. "To do what?"

"To wake me in time to dress and make any other preparations. Are you a Mover?"

"To a degree, although my Seeing powers are greater. I may be called upon for either function tonight."

"You know that I am primarily a Mover," said Wulfston. "If I eat well of the meal you have provided, especially the meat, my body will seek healing sleep, because there is still poison in my blood."

"Poison? Oh, you mean the kleg. It is not a poison, Lord Wulfston. It does no lasting harm. In proper dosage, it inhibits the powers of either a Mover or a Seer."

"It rendered me unconscious, twice," Wulfston reminded him.

Kamas nodded. "In a large dose it does that to anybody. We had to make certain we could capture you the first time, and after you regained consciousness Laruna overdosed you accidentally when the small dose she first gave you did not prevent you from Seeing. We meant you no permanent harm, but Norgu had said you were extremely dangerous."

"I am. But only to those who attack me first."

"Then you *are* a danger to Tadisha."

"No. She feared I had come to attack your people. I mean her no harm—nor you, Prince Kamas. And I understand your situation perfectly."

"What do you mean?"

"You have just reached manhood, but have years yet before you will attain the height of your powers. As a man, you feel you should be a protector to your sister, but because she is older, her powers and experience are greater than yours. There are times when you resent her strength, and times when she resents your efforts to protect her."

Kames stared at him. "How can you know that? Have you some of the Grioka's talent—or are you that great a Seer?"

"Neither." Wulfston laughed. "I'm younger brother to a very powerful Lady Adept!"

For one moment Kamas glared at him—and then broke into a grin. "Just don't tell me things will be better in a few years."

"All right, I won't. But may I tell you that things got better between Aradia and me as our age difference came to mean less an less?"

Kamas nodded thoughtfully. "Yes—at least that's more encouraging than the stuff of legends. Savishna and Shangonu are still fighting, as they have been since the world was new."

"The two gods?" Wulfston asked. "You worship Shangonu, I understand, and the Savishnon—"

"Savishna, the war god. They are gods, of course, and so can take either sex if they have reason to assume a form recognizable to men. But it is said that Savishna is most terrible in the form of an avenging woman. Her warriors declare themselves faithful to her, and will not touch a human woman until they have won the territory she commands them to take. They lost the battle at Johara four years ago, because of a woman, a rival to Savishna. Savishna is not a forgiving god."

"Is Shangonu?" Wulfston asked.

"Yes. He is a builder, Savishna a destroyer. But that is the way of gods. Savishna and Shangonu were born of the Great Mother to be the opposing forces that continue life, for the old and weak must make room for the new and strong. But human brothers and sisters should not be opposing forces . . . and my sister wants you at her Ceremony of Vision. I will do nothing—nor neglect to do anything—to oppose her desire."

As he had promised, Kamas woke Wulfston before the Ceremony of Vision, and took him to an anteroom of the temple to prepare. They were garbed in plain brown, featureless garments, and Wulfston reluctantly handed Lenardo's ring over to an attendant, who had also taken Kamas' chain and pendant. Then they paused to wash faces, hands, and feet before entering the temple itself.

The temple was a part of the castle, with the castle wall as its front wall, allowing the people of the city to enter for worship. Tonight, however, that door was closed and barred.

Wulfston had seen screens and benches piled up in hallways and anterooms they had passed through on their way here; obviously at times the huge temple was divided with colorful hangings into smaller areas, and worshipers could sit on benches for the ceremonies. Now, though, the temple was empty except for a low round dais in the center, amid a circle of flaming candles set in high wooden holders. Their light flickered across images painted on the ceiling high above, but Wulfston could not make them out.

At the very center of the ceiling, directly above the dias, a circular hole revealed the stars above.

The room could have held hundreds of people. Tonight

there were only five: Tadisha, Ashuru, Kamas, Barak, and Wulfston. Wulfston and Kamas silently approached from one side, Ashuru, Tadisha, and Barak from the other. All wore the same plain brown garments.

As they entered the circle of candlelight, they stepped up onto the platform, which appeared to be wood covered with the same plain brown cloth as their robes. Tadisha stepped to the center, the other four around her.

Ashuru said, "This is a Ceremony of Vision, a Seeking to know what the presence of Lord Wulfston of the Savage Empire means to the state of Africa. Shangonu guide us to a true Vision, and protect my daughter while her spirit wanders under his guidance."

Tadisha bowed to her mother, and received her kiss on the forehead. Then she turned from Ashuru and sank into the cross-legged position used by Readers and Adepts for concentration. Ashuru was now behind Tadisha, Wulfston directly in front of her, facing the Karili queen. Barak was on Tadisha's right side, Kamas on her left.

The four who were standing joined hands, as Ashuru said, "We form a circle of protection for Tadisha. Once we are seated, that circle must not be broken. Lord Wulfston, do you understand?"

"I understand," he replied. "We must not break the circle."

Ashuru's eyes glittered in the candlelight so that he could not read them, but she was apparently satisfied—perhaps because with her Seer's powers she could tell that this experience was not so alien to Wulfston as he had expected it to be.

The setting was different, the people were different, but the sense of shared energy he felt as they clasped hands was exactly the same as he had known time and again working with Lenardo, Torio, Julia—

The four let go of each other's hands, but the sense of energy suspended between them remained as they stepped back.

Tadisha sank onto the platform, lying on her back, carefully smoothing her robe beneath her so that nothing would cut off her circulation.

When Ashuru, Kamas, and Barak settled into the cross-legged position that could be held for hours without fatigue, Wulfston did likewise, sitting at Tadisha's feet. She lay prone, relaxed, eyes closed.

Wulfston had seen the process a hundred times before, but always the moment when the Reader's face went slack, as if she had gone into a coma, disturbed him. *Reading* Tadisha's personality suddenly disappear, he discovered, was even worse.

He composed himself, expecting a long wait. But only a few minutes passed before Tadisha's eyes opened again and she quickly sat up. She looked around the circle, confused. Then her eyes fastened on Wulfston's.

The eyes were still green, but they blazed with the light of hatred.

It was not Tadisha!

To his horror, he realized that no one else was reacting. Ashuru, Barak, Kamas, all remained in a kind of trance, oblivious to the change in Tadisha.

The look she gave him was rabid. Wulfston had once been called upon to destroy a dog with that look in its eyes, an animal he could not control. He had had to kill it.

But he could not kill Tadisha!

What he Read from the creature facing him, though, was a stranger's mind awhirl with fragments of memory . . . and of madness. Incredible emotional agony fed the need to destroy, to kill.

She became unReadable, but not before he realized that the whirlpool of destructive passion could only be— *Z'Nelia!*

He jumped to his feet, and so did Tadisha's body, now a living weapon set to strike him down. A cruel, triumphant smile came to her lips as her arms came up in an unmistakable gesture.

Wulfston braced his Adept powers, hoping all his strength had returned.

"The circle!" cried Ashuru eyes snapping open. "Don't break—" A scream choked off her words as Tadisha's body whirled, lightning streaming from her fingertips as Wulfston Read Ashuru's agony of recognition that this was not her daughter—too late to protect herself!

Ashuru slumped, burned, and Z'Nelia turned back toward Wulfston.

"Mother!" Kamas gasped, and Wulfston left Ashuru to her son's attentions.

Z'Nelia could use all the force she wanted, and know Wulfston dared not retaliate for fear of harming Tadisha!

Wulfston dropped off the platform to the floor, sending out an Adept command to Z'Nelia to sleep.

A fireball nearly singed his scalp.

Tadisha's body was already sleeping; his command had no effect on the evil currently inhabiting it.

Old and feeble as he was, Barak flung himself at Tadisha's body as she stalked toward the edge of the platform, readying to attack Wulfston again.

When the old man got in her way, she tossed him aside with Adept strength. Wulfston heard the crack of fragile bone snapping as the old man hit the stone floor. One of the candlesticks fell over on him, igniting his robe. Wulfston spared a thought to put out the flame—

But now Tadisha towered above Wulfston, a perfect target that he dared not attack! She reached toward him—

He squatted beside the platform, got his hands under the edges, and lifted.

The next fireball burst against the ceiling.

Tadisha's body let out a surprised yelp and fell off the platform hard, arms flailing.

More of the tall candlesticks clattered to the floor.

Wulfston frantically looked for cover.

He dived behind the upturned dais, narrowly evading a bolt of Adept lightning that charred even the stone floor.

He peered around the edge as Tadisha's body lurched to its feet.

Wulfston crouched behind the heavy platform, using Adept strength to roll the unwieldy shield to protect Ashuru and Kamas, who had toppled off when he spilled Z'Nelia.

The dais exploded into fiery shards.

Tadisha's body faltered, staggering to keep its balance, but there was still terrible hatred in the eyes. Both hands slowly came up to point at Wulfston, and he braced his Adept powers, still not knowing how to defend himself without hurting Tadisha's body.

He remembered the image of Norgu, Adept strength used up, killing his father's assassin by flinging the diamond-headed spear with simple muscle power.

Wulfston grabbed for the scattered candlesticks, flinging them one after another at the woman before him. She deflected them, her attention diverted while he thought desperately, needing a solution before he ran out of projectiles or she flung another lightning bolt at him.

Why hadn't she?

And then he saw. Even in light of the few remaining candles he could see Tadisha's face turning an unhealthy yellow. Her body staggered more with each bat at an oncoming candlestick. Her movements became weaker, less coordinated—

Blessed gods! Tadisha is no Lady Adept, no great and powerful Mover. Z'Nelia is draining her strength, killing her! I'm killing her! But if I stop, she'll kill me.

Nonetheless he stopped, realizing even as he did so that there was no longer enough strength in Tadisha's body for Z'Nelia to seize upon to kill him.

He got up, and grasped her by the arms. "Let her go, Z'Nelia!" he demanded. "Get out of Tadisha's body. If you harm her, I promise I will hunt you down and kill you with my own hands!"

The green eyes fixed on his, and the mouth grimaced into a parody of Tadisha's sweet smile. Her hands came up and grasped his arms, nails digging in. "So you do believe in revenge, Beast Lord. You need not hunt for me. We will meet again. And next time, no frail girl will stand between us!"

Suddenly, the hands dropped. Life went out of the eyes and the body slumped backwards. Desperately, Wulfston Read for heartbeat, breathing—and found none.

Chapter Six

*O*pen to Reading as he searched for signs of life in Tadisha's body, Wulfston Read Kamas broadcast a call for help with the full extent of his Seeing powers. The younger man then tried to take Tadisha's body, but Wulfston brushed him aside, laying her carefully on the stone floor and invoking his Adept powers to force her heart to beat, her lungs to expand and contract.

"See to your mother and Barak," he instructed. "Don't move Barak till I can help him, though!"

"Healers are on the way," Kamas assured him. "We must summon Tadisha back to her body."

Wulfston remembered Tadisha insisting that "blood will tell." Never mind the reason; her brother's mind was familiar, a signal she would feel safe in following. "Summon her," he replied. "I will keep her body alive."

Kamas knelt beside his sister, concentrating. Wulfston wanted to join Kamas in Reading for her wandering spirit, but dared not, for each time he stopped pumping her lungs and heart they stopped functioning.

Unwanted memory reminded Wulfston that when Master Clement had been lost on the planes of existence his body had continued to function. What was there in Africa that threatened Seers who left their bodies? Did Z'Nelia control it, or was she controlled by it? Had she trapped Tadisha, or had the souls of both women been captured by some other force?

Wulfston turned his attention to what Kamas was doing,

and Read a strange, tenuous beacon reaching out from the younger man in a tie of blood-kinship. He Read Tadisha in that beacon—and yet not Tadisha, but those characteristics that she shared with Kamas, being of one womb born.

In the warm feeling of fraternal love, Wulfston felt like an intruder. He almost blanked out of the rapport when he felt—

Tadisha's presence! Gratefully, she reached for her brother and followed him back, her spirit reentering her body.

Once in her body, though, Tadisha lost consciousness.

Where were those healers? Wulfston was just drawing breath to ask Kamas when Tadisha's chest rose and fell. Her heart fought the steady rhythm Wulfston had imposed, and he let it beat wildly for a moment, until it settled into a fast but even tempo.

Tadisha coughed, then moaned. "Lie still!" Wulfston told her.

Her green eyes opened, dilated with fear. "I . . . I can't See!" She tried to lift a hand to her face, and gasped in pain.

"That's why you must lie still," Wulfston explained. "Let me heal you, Tadisha." He concentrated on encouraging the healing force of Tadisha's own body, but she had little energy left for him to work with.

"What happened?" she asked weakly. "Why did you move my body?"

"It wasn't us," Kamas said grimly. "While you were on another plane, Z'Nelia took over your body and attacked us."

Tadisha's eyes widened in astonishment. "She can do that? And rob me of my Seeing powers?"

"It's temporary," Wulfston assured her. "Z'Nelia used the energy of your body. Let me put you into healing sleep, Tadisha. That will rid you of your pain, and a few days of rest and food will restore your powers."

"No—I must tell—" She tried to sit up, but fell back with a moan of pain and frustration. "Where is Mother?"

"Unconscious. Kamas, where are those healers?!"

Kamas focused his Seeing beyond his sister, beyond the temple. Wulfston had had to restrain his Adept powers to battle Z'Nelia in Tadisha's body; his Reading was still good enough to follow Kamas' mind out into the palace.

Everyone was asleep!

Guards lay crumpled at their posts; Seer-priestesses in brown robes slumped in a circle in a small chapel nearby. The healers Kamas had summoned were in another ante-room, lying in attitudes that told Wulfston the Movers had been pacing in impatient concern, waiting and fearing to be called to the temple.

Wulfston surmised, "Z'Nelia must have put everyone into Adept sleep before she attacked us. Tadisha, you are more Seer than Mover. She didn't realize how much of your energy she would expend on that task. She didn't have enough left to kill me."

"So my call was not answered," said Kamas. "I must waken the healers." He started to rise.

A moan of agony came from behind him.

"Mother!" Tadisha put her hand on he brother's arm, without a wince of pain this time, Wulfston noted. At least her body had power to heal that much.

The pain of Ashuru's burns was pulling her toward consciousness. Wulfston quickly sent her into Adept sleep, and started the healing process. It would keep her pain at bay for the time being, but she needed his concentration on the worst of her injuries, and then healing sleep.

He opened as wide as he could to Reading. A wave of pain assaulted him from Barak. "Kamas," he said, "I need your help! Healing both your mother and Barak will diminish my Seeing powers. Come use yours to help me."

"We need the healers," the boy insisted.

"I will waken them," Tadisha said, struggling to her knees.

"Tadisha!" Kamas protested.

"I have no powers now!" she spat like a determined

kitten hissing defiance at a bewildered hound. "Help Wulfston heal Mother and Barak. The palace is vulnerable to attack. I can do no good here, so I will go wake the guards."

"Come," said Wulfston to Kamas, recognizing that Tadisha assessed her responsibility correctly. The girl rose unsteadily, but moved purposefully toward the door, every bit the queen she would be one day.

Kamas knelt reluctantly beside Wulfston, by Ashuru's body. Wulfston found that healing when he could Read through another's greater powers was even easier than being guided by a Reader's words. Soon Ashuru was in healing sleep, and they turned to Barak, drawing his broken bones into alignment, and starting them knitting rapidly. Because these people must be returned quickly to health, Wulfston had to use his own energy in the healing. When the healers finally joined them, Kamas pulled an exhausted Wulfston to his feet.

"Thank you," the younger man said. "Without your help, all of us might have died."

"Without me," Wulfston replied, "there would have been no opportunity for Z'Nelia to attack . . . and perhaps no reason. Where is Tadisha now? I don't know if she can achieve healing sleep alone."

"You're almost asleep yourself!" Kamas pointed out.

"I have reserves of energy," Wulfston replied. "It's part of Adept training. I could heal myself if there were need, but there isn't."

By this time, though, Wulfston could hardly follow Kamas' Seeing, and could Read almost nothing for himself. Tadisha, they found, had sensibly gone to her room, and was sound asleep in her own bed. "She burns with Shangonu's fire," said Kamas. "It is well."

"Healing sleep," Wulfston identified. So Tadisha had enough of the Mover's power that her body could call up that state—as Wulfston's body yearned to do after the long, tense night. Dawn was breaking. He forced himself to stay awake long enough to eat, then went to his own bed, and fell helplessly into dreamless slumber.

//Wulfston! Wulfston, wake up!//

"Mmpf?"

Then he realized that the voice was in his head.

//Who—?//

//Wulfston, what happened? Why are you sleeping in the middle of the afternoon?//

//Lenardo!//

Wulfston sat up, wide awake. //Lenardo, has something happened to you?//

//No, but something has to you. Careful—let me control our Reading. I can keep the Seers from listening in. Why is everyone in healing sleep?//

Wulfston started to tell him, verbalizing, but felt Lenardo pick up the whole memory from his mind at once. //You must teach me how to do that!//

//You'll learn it. Your Reading has improved overnight. You gave control over to me the way a Magister Reader might. Subtlety and control are much harder to learn than distance.//

//I always knew I ought to be a Reader. But you have information for me.//

He "heard" Lenardo's pleased laughter. //Very good— but the news isn't. A message just arrived from Norgu: the survivors of the wreck of the *Night Queen* are to be sold to the slavers in Ketu.//

//Norgu has them?//

//Just the sailors. I still haven't located Zanos or Astra.//

//Huber?//

//No, not Huber either, although I have tried. Contrary to your exaggerated opinion of my powers, I cannot Read the entire continent of Africa.//

Nor could he Read across the sea to home, although he confessed to Wulfston that he had tried. //I worry about Aradia. If I dared go out of body, I would try to Read to

Zendi. At least I hope she has gone there. I want her under Master Clement's care.//

Wulfston told him of trying to send Aradia a letter from Freedom Island. //I don't know whether my request will be honored, or whether the coins were pocketed and the letter thrown away.//

//If Aradia receives it, at least she will know we reached Africa alive.//

//I will send a letter from here before we set out,// Wulfston assured him. //Tadisha will know a trustworthy messenger.// Then he asked, //Out of body . . . could you really Read all the way home?//

There was a long mental silence. Then Lenardo replied, //I don't think so, Wulfston. But if I get the chance, I'm certainly going to try!//

But at the moment their concerns were there in Africa. //Can you help the *Night Queen* crew escape?// Wulfston suggested. //All of you get out together?//

//They don't know I'm here. None of them are Readers, and Norgu has me locked up and guarded.//

//Why is Norgu suddenly selling them?//

//Because you want them,// Lenardo replied. //I can't predict that boy's moves. He has too much strength, and he acts on impulse—like giving my ring to you and telling you I was dead.//

Wulfston started. In the turmoil after Z'Nelia's attack, he had forgotten Lenardo's ring. But he quickly discovered it now lay gleaming on the table beside his bed. He picked it up and slid it back onto his finger. //Yes—he had to know I'd find out he was lying.//

//But not so soon. He wants you to come to him, Wulfston.//

//Oh, I plan to! I'll get you out of there. Where's Ketu?//

//Between here and the Karili castle. You can liberate the *Night Queen* crew on the way—if someone else doesn't buy them first. White men are considered exotic in Africa.//

//Norgu may be cleverer than we give him credit for,//

Wulfston realized. //He can't hold you long, so he's trying to force my hand. Lenardo, I'll get there as soon as I can. Don't try to escape on your own. Although you're conspicuous in Africa, I don't want to have to hunt for you. I'm not that good a Reader yet.//

//You don't think I could track *you* down?// Lenardo asked with mild amusement.

//Of course you could, but why complicate matters? Let me come to you. Once the two of us are in the same place, no one in Africa can stand against us!//

Lenardo agreed. //But Wulfston, if you were a trained Reader, I would not have been able to waken you today.//

//Why? Oh—I remember. Readers are not supposed to Read while they're asleep so they won't intrude on anyone or broadcast anything.// A prickle of fear went through him. //What am I going to do? I have to sleep!//

//Aradia automatically braces her Adept powers when she sleeps,// said Lenardo. //Apparently you don't have the same instinct, but can't you do it consciously?//

//Yes,// Wulfston replied in relief. But what of all the time he had slept, drugged and undrugged, since his Reading had begun, all the strange dreams, the fragments of thoughts and memories? Who could tell what Seers might have been listening in?

When Lenardo withdrew, Wulfston got up and dressed, testing both his Adept and his Reading powers. He felt normal. In fact, he felt positively good. There were no guards on his room, but the castle was battle-ready. It was exhilarating not to have to leave his room to discover that; he could Read into every part of the castle, out into the courtyard, and to the city beyond. He didn't "see" what he Read, but sensed it in a way he could not have explained in words.

Having "seen" the visions produced by Norgu and Barak, he now understood the difference between ordinary Reading an what the Readers called "visualization," a higher-order skill. He wondered if he would ever develop that, or would always be dependent on a better Reader for visualization.

Interesting that in Africa the word for Reader meant "Seer." He must ask Tadisha whether that meant that the ability to visualize was what distinguished someone with minor powers from someone who might command respect—and power.

At the thought of Tadisha, he Read her room, but it was empty. His conscience prodded him: Readers observed strict rules of privacy. The problem was, not having been a Reader before, he had never learned them! However, he chided himself, Reading into people's private rooms was certainly forbidden except in an emergency.

Restricting himself to the public rooms of the castle, he found Tadisha in a small dining room off the kitchen, Traylo and Arlus on either side of her, begging for tidbits. //Tadisha?//

//Lord Wulfston,// she acknowledged. //Won't you join me? I woke up as hungry as a Mover!//

So had he, so he hurried down the stairs. //Your Seeing powers are back.//

//Not yet back to normal, but returning,// she told him.

When Wulfston entered the dining room, Traylo and Arlus came running to meet him, fawning on him as if they had been waiting desperately for his appearance rather than perfectly content with Tadisha.

The Karili princess looked tired, her eyes puffy as if she still needed sleep. She was wearing a silk caftan in shades of green and tan, and her hair was tied back with a scarf of the same material.

She was eating bread and fruit, but only picking at a savory stew whose aroma had Wulfston's mouth watering. "You need the meat," he told her. "The weakness of your body will blunt your Seeing more than meat will. After your strength returns you can go back to eating like a rabbit if you want to." He followed his own advice, helping himself to a liberal portion of the stew. "How are your mother and Barak?"

"Still healing," she replied. "Our scouts confirm what Norgu showed us of the Savishnon—they are ready to move. The members of the Assembly are returning to their own lands to ready their armies."

"And that is why you are up," Wulfston observed. "It's all your responsibility until your mother is well." He was painfully reminded of Aradia taking over rule of their lands, when their father slid inexorably into coma.

"Yes," Tadisha replied simply.

"Let Kamas do it," said Wulfston. "Where is he?"

"Still sleeping. He did not go to bed until he had verified that no one was coming to attack us in our vulnerable state."

"If it's safe for Kamas to sleep, then it's safe for you. You should have had your meal brought to you, Tadisha, and gone right back to sleep."

"I know that now," she replied wearily. "I wouldn't be much good to anyone"— a yawn interrupted her words —"as tired as I still am."

But before Tadisha could find the energy to leave the table, Kamas joined them. He was tense, but otherwise restored, for he had neither been injured nor used Adept powers. "Our healers commend your skill, Lord Wulfston. How is it that a warrior is trained in healing?"

"Isn't that the custom here?" Wulfston asked. "At home, the most powerful Adepts are also the best healers."

"It makes a Mover popular with the people, but it also weakens his powers. You Saw what happened to Norgu's father."

Wulfston smiled sadly. "Unfortunately, most Lords Adept in the Savage Lands felt as you do before our Alliance. We can only hope that the future proves our ways right."

Before he allowed himself to fall asleep that night, Wulfston braced his Adept powers as Lenardo had suggested. If he dreamed, he did not remember it, and in the morning he woke with the sun, refreshed and eager to act.

He would not invade anyone's privacy this morning, so he assumed that Tadisha and Kamas were still sleeping until a servant came to him. "Queen Ashuru is awake, and is consulting with Princess Tadisha and Prince Kamas. She requests that you join them."

Ashuru might be awake, but she was far from well. The superficial burns had healed to skin of a reddish-pink. If left to heal naturally now, with no further Adept stimulus, it would regain its normal color in a few weeks without scarring.

The worst of Ashuru's injuries, though, did not show; she had not left her bed because she could not. Nerves along her spine had been seared. She had little feeling in her legs, and could move her arms only with effort. One of the healers was trying to persuade her to be put back into healing sleep again. "Please, Queen Ashuru—the sooner this kind of injury is healed, the better your chances for complete recovery."

But Ashuru waved the healer aside. "Soon, soon," she promised. "First we must make plans. Lord Wulfston, do you understand what happened in the temple?"

"Z'Nelia entered Tadisha's body while she was out of it," Wulfston replied.

The older woman nodded. "Thank Shangonu, not even a *sabenu* can command a Seer's body once the Seer returns to it. And despite all, my daughter succeeded in her quest."

Tadisha's Vision! Wulfston had completely forgotten it.

Tadisha looked much better today, rested and healthy. "Lord Wulfston," she said formally, "we can no longer blame you for bringing trouble upon us, for it is Shangonu's will that you be here, now, when Savishna rises and Z'Nelia seeks power. I had a True Vision:

"The Savishnon will move inexorably toward the east. Since there is no longer a way directly from their lands to

Z'Nelia's, they will pass through our lands and Norgu's first, destroying as they go. If we mass our armies and deploy our powers against them, we can hold them to the north—for now."

"Why is there no way from the Savishnon lands into Z'Nelia's?" asked Wulfston.

"The road is gone," Kamas replied.

"Gone? Where?" Wulfston asked. "You can't take away a road. You can temporarily block a pass with an avalanche; you can tear down bridges; you can flood a valley the road passes through. But with Adept powers it's easy enough to clear away rubble, rebuild bridges and dams. Z'Nelia's people have had four years to do so."

"The Dead Lands," Ashuru said grimly, "lie in the path the Savishnon would have to take to reach Johara from the north."

"I see," he replied.

Ashuru continued, "Lord Wulfston, do you understand why it is not always possible to obtain a Vision of what one seeks—or why such Visions are often incomplete?"

"Yes," he replied, having been privy to much discussion on the matter after Torio developed the rare gift of prophecy. "The future is affected by both the past and the present. It appears that some events are fated—the will of the gods, the Aventines would say. No matter how we try to stop them, those events happen. The fall of Tiberium was such an event.

"True prophecies concern only such events, which are often foretold many years before they occur. But they are not detailed." He was staring at his hands as he spoke, and suddenly Lenardo's ring came into focus. "The design on this ring," he continued, "represents a prophecy. 'In the day of the white wolf and the red dragon, there will be peace through all the world.' All *our* world, at any rate, for the white wolf is Aradia, my sister, and Lenardo is the red dragon. Their union represents the unity we have achieved, Readers and Adepts together. And there is peace."

He could not voice the thought that forced itself, unbidden, into his mind. *The prophecy does not say how long that day will last. If I don't bring Lenardo back to Aradia—*

"Yes," said Ashuru, "prophecies and Visions give only part of the information we would like to know, for all the rest depends on events and decisions that change from day to day. Tadisha's Vision told that you will play a key role in the upcoming battle, Lord Wulfston. What it did not tell was who will win."

Tadisha spoke. "The battle will be between the greatest forces ever raised on our continent, and you will be a central figure. That battle will change the fate of Africa."

Wulfston asked, "What do you mean by 'central figure'? Or 'changing the fate of Africa'? Where does Z'Nelia fit in? Because I'm here, will the Savishnon be defeated? Or—?"

Ashuru interrupted with a snort of laughter. "If we could answer that kind of question, we would be gods ourselves."

Then what good did it do to put Tadisha in such danger? He did not voice the question, although he suspected that Ashuru Saw it despite her weakened condition. If she did, she pretended not to. "So," she said, "you are a part of our battle plan, whether we want you or not. Shangonu protect us all."

"I will help you all I can," he replied. "But first I must ask your aid. The crew of my ship are to be sold at the slave market at Ketu. So that I may rescue them, I ask an escort who knows the land, the language, the customs."

"And has money to buy your men," added Ashuru.

Buy them? Before he could protest he realized she was right—the simplest solution was best. "Thank you," he replied. "I will repay you, of course."

"There will be no need for repayment," Ashuru replied. "Either you will lead us to victory, in which case payment is trivial, or you will lead us to our death. And no debts can be repaid to the dead."

"I will take you to Ketu, Lord Wulfston," said Kamas.

"I will go too," Tadisha added. "We must move our armies into position against the Savishnon, and we have promised to help you rescue Lord Lenardo. I am well enough to travel. Mother requires much more healing—"

"With the permission of your healers, Queen Ashuru," Wulfston said, "I will add my powers to speed your recovery."

"Your help is accepted," said the healer, "if the queen permits."

Ashuru nodded; she was growing weaker.

"One more thing," said Wulfston. "I must question Barak. His wounds ought to be healed by now."

"You forget his great age," said the healer. "But you may speak with him when we waken him to give him nourishment this evening."

Ashuru struggled to stay awake. "What else do you think Barak can tell you?"

"The rest of the story of Z'Nelia," he replied.

"Then," Ashuru said, her voice weakening, "I must be here. Tadisha—" She groped weakly in her daughter's direction, and Tadisha grasped her hand. "Promise me. Make the healers wake me, too."

Tadisha looked to the healer, who gave a fatalistic shrug. "I promise, Mother."

Ashuru drifted off, going automatically into healing sleep. If they had had time to spare, Ashuru could have recovered eventually at this rate. But they did not have that time. Wulfston spent the next two hours joining his powers to those of the healer, aiding Ashuru's body to heal.

That evening Wulfston, Tadisha, Kamas, and Ashuru gathered at Barak's bedside. The Grioka watched them warily. "What do you seek of me now? I have Told all I know."

"I think not," Wulfston replied. "In fact, you lied to us."

He heard Tadisha's sharp gasp—obviously one did not

speak so to a Grioka—but Barak appeared more fearful than offended.

"You told us," Wulfston continued, "that after the battle at Johara four years ago, you left as soon as the lava had cooled. I do not think a Grioka would do that. The story was not complete. You would have waited until Z'Nelia either died or recovered. She recovered, and I think what you discovered the next time you were in her presence sent you into exile."

Barak nodded. "Blood will tell, Lord of the Black Wolf. You will not let me keep my secrets any more than Z'Nelia would. It is true—driven by a Grioka's need to know the end of the story, I stayed in Johara while Z'Nelia's spirit wandered . . . and returned. Once she was well, I sought audience to my sorrow.

"I learned what truly happened on Mount Manjuro, when Z'Nelia released the fire demon. What I did not expect, though, was that Z'Nelia learned my greatest secret as well.

"Z'Nelia had always been a most powerful Mover, with little ability to See. She returned from the land of the dead with her Seeing powers increased manyfold. She Saw my betrayal of her father, many years before.

"It was not long after the Aresh, the Time of Change," Barak replied to Wulfston's look of confusion, "when the first Movers and Seers appeared in Africa. There were several generations of turmoil, as those with powers overthrew hereditary tribal leaders, and some created new tribes. Often these new leaders would then fight one another. There was war, and for a long time little security for anyone."

"Yes," replied Wulfston. "That was very much the way things happened in the lands where I grew up. Only in my father's generation did some Lords Adept seek peace."

"Nerius was not your father," said Barak. "Listen—I will tell you who you are. In your grandparents' generation there were born in Djahat, the seat of the Zionae before the Savishnon drove them eastward, twin sisters, both extremely powerful Movers. As they grew to womanhood and came into their full powers, it was inevitable that they would both seek the throne—but only one could have it.

"While their father, Nelatu, yet lived and held the throne, both women married men with strong Mover powers, and bore children. Raduna bore a son, and Katalia a daughter. Raduna's son was a powerful Mover, but Katalia's daughter showed only the smallest trace of such power, and no Seeing ability at all.

"To avoid a power struggle for the throne of Djahat at his death, Nelatu declared Raduna his heir, and her son Desak after her. He also arranged marriages for his grandchildren. Desak had just passed his initiation into manhood, and was married to a girl who already showed great Seeing ability. But Katalia's daughter, several years younger than Desak, was betrothed to the son of a distant cousin in whose line neither Moving nor Seeing powers had ever manifested.

"The children were betrothed in the temple of Shangonu, and lived in the palace. They were daily reminded that it was the will of Shangonu that they love one another, and marry when they came of age." Barak gave Wulfston a gentle smile. "It appears that they did not forget."

"My parents?" Wulfston asked. "But how did they come to be slaves in the Aventine Empire?"

"When Nelatu died, the throne passed peacefully to Raduna—but then came the Savishnon hordes. Raduna and her husband died in the battle for Djahat, and the Zionae were driven eastward, to take refuge in the mountains near Johara. Desak was powerful, but still very young; Katalia and her husband saw an opportunity to seize the throne from their nephew before he came to his full powers.

"At that time, over fifty years ago, I was newly Grioka. I had completed my apprenticeship, learned all the old tales, and was beginning to Tell my own. I watched the palace being built at Johara, and Told the old tales to Desak, who liked me because I was also young, and eager to Tell of adventure.

"Yes," Barak sighed, "I was young . . . and foolish. Griokae should stand outside their Tales, never involve themselves. Yet when I knew that Katalia was plotting against Desak, what was I to do? He was the rightful King of the Zionae, Nelatu's chosen heir. I . . . told him. I earned his gratitude, and his trust.

"And I learned why Griokae must never become involved. Desak pretended he did not know of the plot against him. He invited his aunt and uncle, and his cousin and her betrothed, to a family dinner—where his Seers revealed their plot! Katalia and her husband were helpless, for Desak had laced their food with kleg. He slaughtered them, before the eyes of their daughter and her betrothed.

"The children were, technically, still that: in the next year, both would have undergone initiation into adulthood, and then been permitted to marry by Zionae law. But on that day they were still children, innocent under our law even if they had known of their elders' plot, which they did not. I knew that, and told Desak so, staying his hand when he would have struck down his cousins as well.

"I persuaded Desak that his position was precarious enough without slaying two defenseless children. Yet he feared the girl, for Nelatu's blood ran in her veins, and he saw in her or her children a future threat. He wanted the two dead, but would not kill them himself, so he charged their execution to the one man he thought he could trust."

"You," said Wulfston.

Barak nodded. "I could not kill them, but I could not allow them to remain in Africa, either. It is an evil thing to sell another into slavery, but it was all I could think of to preserve both those children's lives and the unity of the Zionae nation." He smiled sadly. "But Shangonu's plans are not to be so lightly thwarted. The confrontation was merely postponed, for here you are, the son of those two children, returned to fight Z'Nelia for the throne of the Zionae."

"I don't want the throne of the Zionae."

"Z'Nelia will never believe that. That is why she has tried repeatedly to kill you."

"How does she know who I am, when until now I didn't know myself?"

"When she Saw my betrayal of Desak, she knew your parents had survived. And the moment she Saw you she must have known, as I did, who you are. What other pure Zionae, with great Mover's powers, would come from the northern lands?"

As if out of nowhere, a question formed in Wulfston's mind. "What is the meaning of 'Kana la sabenu Z'Nelia'?"

Tadisha gasped. "Where did you hear that?"

"On Freedom Island, from a drunken man who tried to kill Chulaika. What does it mean?"

It was Barak who answered: " 'Death to the mad witch Z'Nelia.' "

"I might have known," Wulfston said. "Tell me the rest of the story. What happened after you sent my parents away?"

"Desak ruled, violently, impulsively—but he kept the lands of the Zionae as a stronghold against the Savishnon. His wife bore him two daughters, but no sons. Although he feared a repetition of what had happened between his mother and her sister, it happened that Z'Nelia had great Mover's powers, while her sister had none. There was no question as to Desak's heir.

"He chose for Z'Nelia's consort a man who was also a great Mover. It was a political marriage, uniting his daughter with the only Mover with the power to be a threat to the royal family. Desak died soon after Z'Nelia bore a son, and her husband in effect ruled the Zionae for some years—until she approached the peak of her powers. Then came the attack of the Savishnon, and her defeat of them, as you have Seen."

"Z'Nelia's family," Wulfston prompted. "Did she kill them?"

"She meant to kill them. In fact, when she returned from Mount Manjuro to Johara she thought she had. For they betrayed her. Matu—"

"Norgu's father? Norgu is Z'Nelia's son?" Wulfston demanded in astonishment.

Tadisha gasped. "Shangonu protect us! If they should ever unite against us—!"

"Unlikely," said Barak. "Z'Nelia will never trust Norgu again after he turned against her at Mount Manjuro. You see, Matu betrayed Z'Nelia with her own sister. Z'Nelia had grown more powerful than Matu, and he resented it. Their son, Norgu, showed exceptional powers for so young a child. Her sister had no powers of her own, but saw in Matu's child the chance to gain someone with powers whom she could control. So when he was quarreling with Z'Nelia over who ruled in Johara, she seduced Matu, and became pregnant.

"In the face of the Savishnon threat, Z'Nelia pretended to forgive them, claiming that she would welcome the child her sister carried—her own husband's child. But when they went to Mount Manjuro, she used her Mover's powers to topple the faithless couple into the volcano."

"This was four years ago," said Wulfston. "Z'Nelia's sister—can it be Chulaika?"

"That was her name, although it is no longer to be spoken in Z'Nelia's lands."

Wulfston looked to Ashuru, Tadisha, and Kamas. "So *that* is what this is all about! Did you know?"

"No," said Ashuru. "How could we?"

"They could not," Barak affirmed. "It was not to be Told. Not only Z'Nelia—Norgu will kill me if he finds out I have told you."

"Then, since you have told this much," said Wulfston, "you might as well finish the story. Z'Nelia tried to kill Matu and Chulaika at the volcano."

"Norgu loved his father," Barak continued. "When Z'Nelia tried to kill him, Norgu turned against his mother, and she pushed him into the volcano with the others. Norgu and Matu together had the power to save themselves and Chulaika, but Z'Nelia returned to Johara thinking them dead. Matu, Norgu, and Chulaika fled west, and found lands for themselves."

"Chulaika bore Chaiku, and after Matu died she decided to return from the dead to depose her sister," Wulfston finished. "Probably Norgu's growing power made her move now—and drag me into it because she needed someone with strong powers to stand a chance against either Norgu or Z'Nelia." He shook his head, all that he had learned too much to assimilate at once. "Before anything else can happen, I am going to Norgu's castle for Lenardo."

"I will follow as soon as I can ride," the Grioka replied. "That is a tale I will have to know."

"You may ride with me," said Ashuru. "We will be only a day or two behind you, Lord of the Black Wolf."

Ashuru followed their progress on the three-day journey to Ketu, either Kamas or Tadisha reporting to her each evening. Wulfston worried that enemy Seers might listen in, but the messages were only of their own journey, no mention of Ashuru's plan to keep the Savishnon to the north.

There was no further contact from Lenardo. With Norgu back at his castle, the Master Reader was more closely observed, but the lack of contact was another worry.

Letting the army continue toward Norgu's lands, Wulfston accompanied Tadisha and Kamas on the road to Ketu. He let his Karili friends do the Seeing, only occasionally Reading through them. For all he knew, he could be broadcasting "Come and get me!" to Z'Nelia every time he damped his Adept powers to Read something.

As nothing happened—no attacks, nothing either Kamas or Tadisha could See that seemed suspicious—he was feeling rather self-congratulatory as they topped a hill and came in sight of the trade city.

Traylo and Arlus suddenly stopped, their hackles rising, as they snarled at a patch of brush at the side of the road.

"Lord Wulfston, for Hesta's sake, will you call off your dogs?"

He recognized the voice. "Zanos!"

A tall figure came out of the brush, a man dressed in a deep-hooded robe, with long sleeves that covered his hands. The fabric trailed the ground, covering every bit of Zanos' white skin, the hood hiding his head. But when he faced Wulfston he threw the hood back, revealing the familiar freckled face under the thatch of flaming hair.

But the blue eyes were haunted, and there were lines in Zanos' face that told of a man driven.

"Where is Astra?" Wulfston had to ask, although he knew that if Zanos' wife were alive she would be at his side.

"Drowned," was the curt reply. "Old Huber, too. We both tried to reach her when the ship sank. He was closer. The whirlpool that dragged her under took him along."

Wulfston instinctively reached out a hand in attempted comfort. "I'm sorry—" he began.

Zanos shook him off. "I will avenge her," he replied flatly. Then he eyed Tadisha, Kamas, and their retinue. "You've come to get the *Night Queen* crewmen out of the slavers' pens?"

"Yes," said Wulfston, "and then to rescue Lenardo. He's just two days' journey from here. Come and meet my friends, and we will tell you our plans."

They went off the road to where a clear brook meandered through the meadow, and sat and talked as they ate their midday meal. Zanos had been living off the land. He looked gaunt, but Wulfston was not certain how much of that was grief, and how much deprivation. His fair skin was red with sun- and windburn. Under the robe he wore his Aventine tunic, now torn and threadbare. His sandals were also his own, stained with seawater and repaired with rawhide.

"Where did you find a robe long enough for you?" Wulfston asked.

"Haven't you noticed? The people in this land are very tall, like Sukuru."

"The Warimu," Tadisha supplied.

"Yes, of course. Zanos, have you seen or Read any sign of Sukuru or Chulaika? I haven't."

"Read?" asked Zanos. He had been braced to use Adept powers ever since they had encountered him. Now Wulfston felt him drop his defenses to Read him.

//Yes, Read,// he admitted. //Probably at about your level, although I haven't had the opportunity for training or testing yet.//

//Congratulations,// Zanos told him, but there was no joy in the perfunctory courtesy.

//Zanos . . . ?//

The man's haunted blue eyes fixed on Wulfston's. //It was a joy to Read with Astra while she lived. But it became a curse when I suffered her death. She died calling out to me—reaching out to me—and I could not reach her!//

The gladiator's thoughts cut off abruptly. "I will avenge her death," he repeated. "But first I will help you free the *Night Queen* crew. I've been into town. The eight white men reported for sale are definitely Captain Laren's men, but I didn't know how I was going to break them out of there alone."

"Zanos," said Wulfston, "we are going to buy them."

"You will contribute to the slave trade!"

"We need our strength for another battle," said Kamas.

"But slaving is wrong!" Zanos protested. "Bah! You people probably profit by it—but Lord Wulfston, surely you want to destroy the slave pens!"

"Zanos, I do not approve of slavery," Wulfston replied, keeping his temper by recalling that this man had been a slave and would never forget the experience. "But you have to understand that if we call that kind of attention to ourselves in Ketu, we will give ourselves away."

"You've thrown in with them!" Zanos gasped. 'That's why they wanted you in Africa—to help them fight this Z'Nelia."

"There is a war brewing. We could find ourselves friend-less, in the midst of a battle in which we would appear enemies to every side."

Zanos looked down at his hands, then over at Wulfston. "We? You look as if you belong here."

"Only to you," the Lord Adept replied grimly. "I am as much a stranger in Africa as you are, Zanos. It is only by chance that I have made some friends. With their help, I'll have the *Night Queen* crew free by nightfall. If you will not help, at least do not interfere."

Their eyes locked. At last Zanos said, "You know where Lenardo is, and I don't. You are probably right not to call attention to yourself as a Lord Adept. Very well. I will not interfere in your . . . purchase."

Because of the impending war, the market for exotic slaves had dropped. Kamas bought the group of eight white men for what Tadisha said was a fifth of what they would have brought a month before.

When Kamas brought them to Wulfston, their feelings were surprise and relief. "My lord, we should have known you'd find us!" exclaimed Telek, the strong, muscular sailor who had challenged Zanos on board ship. "And have you found Lord Lenardo?"

"He is at Norgu's castle," Wulfston explained.

"Norgu!" exclaimed Telek. "That bastard. He's the one who sold us to the slavers!"

One of the other sailors added, "My lord, we were there, and did not see Lord Lenardo."

"Norgu didn't want you to. But Lenardo is there, all right. I've been in contact with him. Do you know of anyone else who survived? We don't want to leave anyone stranded in Africa."

"No, my lord," said Telek. "It seemed all the others with Adept or Reading powers were killed in the storm."

"As if we were their special targets," Zanos confirmed bitterly.

Nevertheless, it felt so good to speak his native language, to be among people from home, that Wulfston wished they could take the time to share the stories of their adventures. But Lenardo was waiting.

Within the hour they were on the road, the *Night Queen* crew eager to act against the man who had sold them into the slave pens.

They rode until an hour past sunset, then made camp. If they started early the next day, they could get close enough to Norgu's castle that only a short ride the next day would take them there, fresh and ready to fight if necessary. It would probably be necessary; it was unlikely that Norgu did not know there was an army approaching his castle.

Tadisha and Kamas contacted Ashuru, who was on the road now, moving toward them. Her army should join theirs the next day.

They had not yet crossed the border into Norgu's lands, but that border was visible from the hill where they had posted sentries. After the evening meal, Wulfston climbed the hill, trying to Read to Norgu's castle. It was a foolish gesture; he could not Read even as far as he could see from the top of the hill in the moonlight. Was Lenardo Reading their progress? Why didn't he make contact?

Wulfston exchanged passwords with the sentries, then walked down the hill a short way to where someone had felled a tree to form a bench. The view in the moonlight was exquisite, but he was in a little hollow where he could not be seen from above or below; he suspected that this must be a favorite courting spot for young people from the village whose fires twinkled below.

He felt Tadisha's mind touch his, and gave her a wordless welcome. In moments she came to sit beside him.

//Can you See to Norgu's castle from here?// he asked.

"Not without going out of body," she said in a soft voice

that would not carry beyond their sheltered hollow. "You should not be attempting to See it, either. We want Norgu to think our movement is simply positioning our troops against the Savishnon assault. And who knows what Savishnon Seers might make of your thoughts?"

"From what Barak showed us, they simply take anything foreign as something to be destroyed."

"Let's not talk about the Savishnon," said Tadisha, "or Norgu, either. Is your land so beautiful in the moonlight, Lord Wulfston?"

"The moon shines on the whole world," he replied. "Its light reveals beauty everywhere." He turned to look at her face, silvered, with golden glints in those eyes that glowed like a cat's.

She turned her face to his, but before he dared follow his own desire, she leaned toward him, murmuring, "Then you could learn to love this land as much . . ." Her voice trailed off as her lips brushed his, producing almost a spark as he started back.

Tadisha straightened, peering at him. "Wulfston, are you afraid of me?"

"Of you? No. Of another woman trying to control me? I will always be wary of that."

"I'm not trying to control you!" she said indignantly. "I like you!"

"And you would like me to stay in Africa," he observed.

"This is your homeland."

He shook his head. "No, Tadisha. This is the home of my ancestors, but it is not *my* home. I understand now why my parents never wanted to return to Africa; they would not have wanted me here, where Chulaika and Z'Nelia use me as a pawn in their games of power, and you and your mother— I'm tired of women pushing me around!"

Tadisha smiled. "You sound just like Kamas!"

"I understand just what he's going through," he told her seriously. "My parents often left me in the care of my sister until they were killed, and then Nerius took me home and handed me over to Aradia. It's difficult to explain. I don't want you to think I don't love her. I do. And she loves me, but she is only now beginning to accept me as her equal. And I don't know if she'll ever stop trying to manipulate me."

"And you think I am trying to manipulate you?" Tadisha asked. Wulfston heard what sounded like honest amazement in her voice. Then she said thoughtfully, "I must be very careful how I treat Kamas. I would not want his having an older sister with stronger powers to confuse his thinking. I certainly don't want my younger brother to have trouble understanding the difference between manipulation and caring."

Queen Ashuru caught up with them on the road the next day, bringing good news. "The combined army of the Assembly has driven off the first assault of the Savishnon. They have turned eastward, traveling across the plain rather than rampaging through our lands. But such an army needs supplies. When they grow hungry, they will turn southward again. Can there be any hope of gaining Norgu's cooperation?"

"Perhaps," suggested Wulfston, "now that we know why he hates his mother we may persuade him to join us against Z'Nelia."

The next day they reached Terza, the small city grown up around Norgu's castle. No one paid them much attention as they rode up the main street toward the castle walls. Obviously Norgu frequently had distinguished visitors.

But while the streets bustled with morning activity, the castle was strangely quiet. The gates were still closed, and no guards stood watch atop the walls. Drifting high above the castle's turrets Wulfston saw—

No, it can't be! Surely not the eagle he had seen at the lake. Yet curiosity prompted him to try to see through this bird's eyes, for it commanded a view of the entire castle.

At his mental touch, the eagle broadcast such a rupulsion that he was rocked in his saddle. *Obviously not the same bird!*

Yet the memory of seeing through the eyes of that eagle prompted another memory: the view Norgu had given the Assembly of the Savishnon armies. Strange . . . it had been much like the eagle's view, from above. Had Norgu also used an eagle, perhaps this one—?

Tadisha, who had been watching and Reading him, now turned her Seer's powers toward the castle. Wulfston opened his own powers to the full—

Where was Lenardo? Why didn't he greet them?

Tadisha, Ashuru, and Kamas all were Seeing now, for they met no minds guarding against intrusion. Wulfston Read with them the empty courtyard, the gates closed but unbarred, the empty stables—

And inside, empty rooms. No servants, no retainers . . . and no guests.

But in Norgu's main hall, devastation.

The place had been fire-stormed.

Charred and blistered remains of furnishings surrounded a blasted corpse. And Norgu, seated in the midst of the ruin, physically unharmed but mentally blank, his eyes fixed in a glassy stare, seeing nothing.

Chapter Seven

*W*ulfston moved toward Norgu, who was obviously in shock. Ashuru brushed past him. "I'll care for the boy. It's his mind that needs healing."

She was right; people injured physically needed Wulfston's skills. He spared a glance at the corpse to confirm his expectations; it was Sukuru.

Then where were Chulaika and Chaiku? And where was Lenardo? Why had the Master Reader not given a mental call for help?

Traylo and Arlus ran out of the main hall, then back to Wulfston, coaxing him to follow. Unable to Read anything to guide him, he accepted the dogs' direction through the corridors and down a stair that narrowed as it wound into darkness. For the first time, he experienced the Reader's gift of movement without hesitation when there was no glimmer of light to see by.

Norgu's dungeons stank of agony and death. By the time he came to the bottom of the stairs, Wulfston was holding his breath. Why had Traylo and Arlus brought him to this empty place?

He could Read no one there . . . alive.

The dogs, though, whimpered and fussed. Wulfston concentrated on a rushlight on the wall, until it burst into smoky flame. In the dim light he saw two bodies on the floor.

Chulaika and Chaiku, mother and son wrapped in one another's arms.

No spark of life—?

They were breathing! He could see no injury; they appeared merely to be unconscious. Then why couldn't he Read—?

Wulfston grasped Chulaika's shoulder, intending to turn her over.

At the touch, something grabbed at his mind! The more he fought, the more he was dragged into seething chaos. His mental shout to Tadisha and Kamas for help was swallowed up in the maelstrom, along with every thought, every memory, that made him a separate being!

Chulaika, Chaiku, and Sukuru stood before Norgu. Sukuru was defeated, Chuklaika controlling Chaiku's powers to hide her thoughts. Norgu must not find out how much power his half-brother had, or he would either kill the boy or take him from her to use as his own weapon.

For Chaiku was Chulaika's weapon, carefully crafted to use against Z'Nelia. No one was going to take her son from her before the time was ripe!

"I don't care what you do, Sukuru," Norgu was saying. "You're worthless to me. Shall I kill you? You have been of service to me, even though you did not intend it. You might have brought Lord Wulfston, but you also brought me the hostage who will deliver him right into my hands. Wulfston's coming here, thinking to take Lenardo from me as easily as I took him from you."

The young Mover turned his attention to Chulaika. "What do you think, dear aunt, betrayer of my mother? You chose this stranger from a distant land to be your champion. A fine champion! The only way you could get him here was to kidnap his brother. Are your charms fading, Chulaika? Couldn't you seduce the Beast Lord as you did my father?"

Chulaika stood impassively. Let Norgu reveal just how much he knew of her plan. "You'd never help me," she said.

"Why should I share the throne of the Zionae with you and your bastard?" Norgu demanded. "You pinned your hopes on that poor little baby—you thought he'd have my father's powers. But he's just like you, without power, a weakling. He can't even talk! That's the kind of offspring you produce, Chulaika."

Norgu lounged back on his throne in an attitude of disrespect, waiting for Chulaika's response. She refused to give him one. Finally he prodded, "Should I let you go with Sukuru? You'd make a good family. Bunch of weaklings. Maybe I should make you marry him."

Suddenly Norgu sat up straight. "What—?"

His servants were running in the corridor outside the main hall, men dashing up the great staircase toward the room where Lenardo was kept.

Chulaika Saw with Norgu, Lenardo on his feet, braced for the onslaught. The white man had some minor Mover's powers, certainly enough to handle those servants.

But not Norgu! From the young Mover's mind, the command to sleep struck the stranger lord. The man fought it easily until Norgu backed it with his Mover's powers, physically overpowering the Seer. The white man slumped into unconsciousness. The servants entered the room, and began to carry Lenardo out—

Where? Why?

Norgu had seemed surprised when the servants appeared. Yet it must have been on his order.

Chulaika stared at Norgu, and suddenly he turned, fixing his eyes on her.

It wasn't Norgu!

Chulaika's Seer's powers were very dim; she had recognized only the overlay of Norgu up to that moment, but in those eyes she recognized the look, the madness.

Norgu's hand rose clumsily, still fighting the force within his body.

Chulaika screamed and flung herself behind Sukuru, shielding Chaiku with her body.

The thunderbolt struck Sukuru, killing him instantly.

"No!" Norgu howled, fighting the demon in possession of his body.

Chulaika slithered out from beneath Sukuru's charred body and ran, dragging Chaiku by the hand. The boy began to wail in fear. "Quiet!" she hissed, and his sounds stopped, although tears still rolled down his face.

Where could she hide?

Thunderbolts were striking randomly throughout the castle as the witch possessing Norgu improved her control.

Hangings burst into fire, and servants dropped in their tracks.

Chulaika scurried into the kitchen, where a number of Norgu's staff cowered, waiting for orders. "Under the table!" Chulaika told them, diving beneath it herself, clutching Chaiku close. The servants crowded in around them, their terror providing a psychic shield. Chulaika took Chaiku in her arms, calmed him, and entered the mother/son bond in which she could brace her son's Mover's powers. It made them nearly invisible to Seers.

But their attacker had firm control of Norgu's powers now, and was methodically destroying his castle. The kitchen fireplace was large enough to roast a buffalo. When the fire leaped from it to the table, the servants scattered, Chulaika and Chaiku with them.

Carrying her son, Chulaika ran with the servant who spilled out into the hall, until they came to the stairway leading down to the dungeon.

Praying desperately to Shangonu that the intruder had not been able to follow her, she fled down the winding stairs, stumbling in the darkness, catching the rhythm until the stairs ended abruptly and she hurtled into darkness, falling onto a damp stone floor.

Breathless, she clung to Chaiku, making him enforce the Mover's shield with all his strength, a strength amazing for a child so young, but still a child's strength. In moments, the effort dragged them both into unconsciousness.

"Lord Wulfston! Wulfston, come out of it!"

The voice came from a great distance, calling somebody she vaguely knew.

//Let go! Come out of the woman's mind, Wulfston!//

He gasped with the mental anguish of releasing memories that for long moments had been *his*, but Tadisha's mind was there to support him.

He was kneeling, frozen, with his hand on Chulaika's shoulder. Tadisha's warm hand touched his cold one, lifting it from the contact.

The weakness of relief flooded him as he forced himself up on legs gone numb. "Thank you. I'll be all right now."

"What happened?" Tadisha asked. "We couldn't find you! Finally the dogs led me down here."

"The woman is Chulaika," Wulfston replied, staring down at her. She was not veiled now. He had seen that face before, in Barak's vision. "Z'Nelia's twin sister."

Tadisha used her Seeing power to examine the woman and her child. "They're just unconscious. We'll take them upstairs and put them to bed. Which is where you belong, too."

"No." he insisted, "I'm all right now. But Z'Nelia has Lenardo."

"Z'Nelia!"

"She took over Norgu's body, used his powers to destroy his own castle, and put Lenardo into Adept sleep. Apparently she used Norgu's servants to carry Lenardo away—I don't know where, because Chulaika doesn't. But Norgu had the power to do Z'Nelia's will, as your body didn't, Tadisha."

"But what was he doing out of body? Norgu has never shown much interest in expanding his Seer's powers."

"He was not out of body," Wulfston replied. "Z'Nelia has learned to take over a Mover who is awake. That's why

Norgu was in shock when we got here. He couldn't fight her off. It was a harsh lesson, Tadisha, to have his own powers wrested from his control."

"Mother finally brought him out of shock," said Tadisha, "and he is sleeping."

By this time they were up the stairs. Wulfston drew deep breaths of clean air, then asked, "Where is my help needed?"

"We've put the worst injured in the main hall."

There were the usual casualties of Adept attack: burns, broken bones, shock. Within hours, all were in healing sleep, and those uninjured had already buried the dead, as was the custom here. Wulfston, Tadisha, Kamas, Barak, and Ashuru met around the dining table.

When Ashuru heard what Wulfston had learned from Chulaika's memories, she said, "We are in grave danger indeed. Z'Nelia's powers grow daily. Perhaps she is now stronger than all of us together. Yet if we do nothing to stop her, she may learn more and yet more, becoming ever more powerful."

"She seeks a confrontation with me," said Wulfston, "or she would not have taken Lenardo. She must think I'm here to take her throne. If only she understood that I don't want it! If we had found Lenardo here today, he and I would have helped you against the Savishnon, and then gone home. Now I must fight Z'Nelia for Lenardo. I ask your aid."

"You have it," said Ashuru. "Z'Nelia made herself my enemy when she attacked my daughter."

But Chulaika and Norgu were another matter. Z'Nelia's sister and her son were awake the next morning, and Wulfston confronted them with all he had learned from the unexpected mental contact. "You were the real force in the plan to bring me to Africa," he told her, "not Sukuru. You merely used him to keep my attention from you, so I would not find out that you are Z'Nelia's sister."

"Since I have no powers of my own," Chulaika replied, "why would I try to oppose Z'Nelia?"

"Ah, but you have a power," Wulfston told her, "a unique power in my experience, and, I suspect, that of the Movers and Seers here as well. That is why you have been able to hide . . . your ability to direct the powers of others!"

Pure fury burned in Chulaika's eyes. Wulfston saw her glance at Barak. Now her secret was a part of history.

He, too, looked to the Grioka, asking a silent question. "Go on," the old man said. "I think, Lord Wulfston, that you have something of the Grioka's talent yourself."

"If so," said Wulfston, "I haven't known how to use it. I should have known you were lying, Chulaika, that day on Freedom Island. You made us all think the man with the knife was attacking Chaiku. But no matter how drunk he was, why would he publicly attack a little boy? He was just drunk enough to See and yet not think. Yes, a minor Seer, who suddenly Saw through your veil the face of his enemy, Z'Nelia!"

Chulaika stared defiantly, refusing to acknowledge Wulfston's analysis.

" 'Death to the mad witch Z'Nelia,' " he quoted, taking grim pleasure in watching her eyes widen in frustration. "You lied to me about what he said. And you let me think that I misjudged my powers and killed him—but *you* killed him, with Chaiku's power."

"That's nonsense," said Chulaika. "My son is only three years old."

"The age I was when my powers first manifested," Wulfston replied. "A three-year-old could not direct his small strength to kill, but a well-practiced grown woman could. I should have recognized what was wrong with that picture. By maternal instinct you should have shielded Chaiku with your own body, as you did yesterday against Z'Nelia's attack. But you held him in *front* of you, using his powers against that man who was too drunk to realize

that it couldn't possibly be Z'Nelia he perceived beneath
your veils!"

Wulfston studied Chulaika's face. "Did you really think
you could take over my powers, direct them as you pleased?
That was your plan, wasn't it? The latest of your plans to
steal the throne from Z'Nelia. First you seduced Matu,
knowing that the people loved him better than Z'Nelia.
You thought you might get him to kill her, and marry you.

"But before you dared propose that plan, you became
pregnant with Matu's child. That gave you something to
hold over him—a rival to Z'Nelia's son, and a potential
Mover to protect you if your plans for his father failed.

"Then came the Savishnon. What really happened on
Mount Manjuro, Chulaika? Z'Nelia knew about your treachery and Matu's, and pushed you into the volcano. She
didn't count on Norgu's love for his father, did she? I
wonder if either you or your sister knows anything about
love.

"Norgu saved your life. Matu alone could not have
saved both you and himself. You found yourself not only
with the man you wanted and his unborn child—but with
Matu's son by Z'Nelia! That must have been a happy
family group.

"You pretended it was, didn't you? But Matu and Norgu
became closer as Matu trained his older son. You decided
to get rid of them both. Wasn't that your plan, the day the
three assassins attacked? You let everyone assume Z'Nelia
sent them. Did you perhaps pose as your sister, so that
the assassins themselves thought Z'Nelia directed them?

"No matter. Matu was killed, but Norgu revealed the
strength of his powers. He never suspected you; he always
assumed Z'Nelia killed Matu. You knew he would eventually seek to depose his mother, but you felt that Chaiku,
as Matu's son and with Mover's powers, had the right to
the throne.

"But Norgu was far older and stronger; to use Norgu
and Z'Nelia against one another, you had to move when

Norgu did, long before Chaiku was old enough to be effective in battle. Then you heard the story about me, hired Sukuru. And we know the rest.

"Except," he added slowly, distastefully, "that you have used your child's own powers to keep him from learning to talk, to keep that poor little boy from accidentally telling someone of the games you play with him, the things you make him do."

Chulaika's skin grew ashen with shock as her secrets were revealed. She clutched Chaiku, but she did not try to attack. What use would it be?

Ashuru spoke. "Chulaika, as a mother I cannot but abhor you. Yet we have in common the desire to depose Z'Nelia, for her powers are combined with madness. We cannot trust you—so what are we to do about you?"

"We could," said Wulfston, "simply turn her over to Norgu, with the evidence that she, and not Z'Nelia, killed his father."

Chulaika's eyes widened. "No! He would kill me, and my baby, too. Or else he would use Chaiku horribly—"

"Worse than you have used him?" Ashuru demanded.

"I'll help you!" Chulaika pleaded. "I *know* Z'Nelia—we are twins. Loving her, Matu had no choice but to love me. And our powers—she has the power, and I have the control. If I can only get close enough, I can control Z'Nelia! I can make her turn her powers against herself. Just don't betray me to Norgu!"

For the moment Wulfston agreed with Ashuru: it was best not to tell Norgu of Chulaika's treachery. He and the Karili queen shared the same misgivings, but, "Despite how Chulaika has used him," Ashuru said, "Chaiku is better off with his mother than with Norgu. If that boy were to gain further power now, before he has learned to use wisely what he has . . . " She shook her head sadly.

"You are right," said Wulfston. "Besides, we need Norgu's help against both Z'Nelia and the Savishnon. When all is over, something will have to be done about Chaiku. He cannot be left unprotected once his powers are recognized. But for now—"

Ashuru nodded. "His best protection until we have somehow dealt with Z'Nelia is the one his mother has given him: silence."

So Wulfston was left to approach Norgu, who had already recovered his physical powers, like any other Adept who had used them to the limit. Emotionally, though, the boy was a seething cauldron. "I will never forgive Z'Nelia! I will kill her!"

Wulfston tried to hide his concern at Norgu's agitation. "We will all fight Z'Nelia together. Consider what happened here: alone, you are no match for her. But you can join your powers to mine and those of the Movers Ashuru has brought. Let the Seers use their powers of mind to aid us against Z'Nelia. Only by working together do we have a chance to defeat her."

"I want to kill her with my own hands," Norgu said. "I will drive my spear through her heart!"

Wulfston curbed his exasperation, and said reasonably, "She will not allow you that close. Think, Norgu. If you approach her alone, with only your own people, she will do exactly what she did here: take over your body and turn you into a weapon against yourself. Our only possible safety is in numbers, Movers and Seers attacking her together."

Norgu's face was wrenched into a pouting scowl. "She is my mother. I have the right to her throne. I am her heir."

"Then act like the heir to the throne, a leader among men," Wulfston suggested. "Take the opportunity to gain strong allies. Let us go ahead of you," he added, lest Norgu should decide to lead the attack, "while you remain as the secret weapon. We will approach Johara first, Movers and Seers attacking Z'Nelia with all our powers. When she is distracted, you launch your attack, and allow me to go in and rescue my brother under cover of your unexpected powers."

"Z'Nelia is not in Johara," Norgu said flatly.

"What?"

"She is in our ancestral home in Djahat, ancient seat of the Zionae nation, just three days' journey from here."

"I thought the Savishnon held Djahat."

"They did after they drove my ancestors out, until my mother defeated them. My father and Chulaika and I fled through those Savishnon-held lands after the battle at Johara. With Savishnon between us and Z'Nelia, we felt safe in the lands of the Warimu, but with the Savishnon weakened other peoples moved into those lands, driving the remaining Savishnon northward. A short time ago, Z'Nelia took those lands into Zionae power once more. Now I know she knew where I was, and wanted a common border between our lands."

"Then," Wulfston wondered, "has she taken Lenardo to Djahat?"

"Yes," Norgu replied, "or at least that was her plan when she stole him from me. I must take my revenge, but you are right. Alone I would have to wait until my powers grew stronger. With your help, I can seek revenge now, before Z'Nelia's madness does any further damage!"

Wulfston refrained from commenting further; he had what he wanted, and could only hope that with the help of Ashuru, Tadisha, and Kamas, Norgu could be kept to their plan.

When he told Ashuru and Tadisha the news, Ashuru said, "I did not think anyone could talk Norgu out of his revenge."

"He still plans revenge; he is just facing the fact that he doesn't have the strength to fight Z'Nelia alone."

Ashuru shook her head. "I had hoped to take him beyond mere acceptance of facts. I failed to heal the wounds left by his mother's treachery—and, of course, his father's. Norgu is obsessed with Z'Nelia's power-madness, yet incapable of recognizing his own."

"But . . . you have the capability to heal such madness?"

"I have the knowledge," Ashuru replied, "but not the time. Norgu needs years of care to counteract his terrible childhood. He is in desperate need of the teaching his father was giving him when he died. If we succeed against Z'Nelia—"

"—Norgu will expect to take her throne," said Tadisha. "How are we to prevent him?"

"Wait," said Wulfston. "Queen Ashuru, can your Seers not work together to heal sick minds quickly, as our Master Readers do at home?"

"Quickly?" she asked. "If you mean weeks or months instead of years, yes. But if you mean that I should attempt to heal Norgu before—"

"Not Norgu," said Wulfston. "Z'Nelia."

"What?!" Both women spoke at once, two pairs of green eyes fixed on him.

"We have all been assuming," he explained, "that if we win the upcoming battle, it will mean Z'Nelia's death. That would create a power struggle between the Karili Assembly and Norgu over rule of the Zionae lands, with the Savishnon ever available to take advantage of any weakness. But what if we do not kill Z'Nelia, but *heal* her?"

"How do we control her in the battle, so that we can have the chance to heal her?" Ashuru asked. "Tadisha will be a powerful Seer one day, but she has neither the power nor the training to help me with Z'Nelia now."

Wulfston looked into the lion's eyes. "Lenardo has both."

"Can you speak for him?"

"If he is conscious he will be Reading. The moment he knows what you intend to do, I know he will aid you."

Ashuru nodded. "Yes—from what I have Seen of Lenardo in your mind, I know that you speak truthfully. But can you give a promise for him, and bind him to it?"

"What do you mean?" Wulfston asked warily.

"Suppose we win the battle, and free Lenardo. Will he

stay in Africa as long as it takes to heal Z'Nelia so that she can be trusted on the throne?"

If only I could ask him! Wulfston thought, remembering Aradia, pregnant—but surrounded by Readers and Adepts.

"Perhaps," Tadisha answered his thought, "I can reach along the road to Johara out of body. Men on horseback couldn't have ridden that far yet. If Lord Lenardo is conscious—"

"I doubt he's being taken to Johara," Wulfston remembered, no longer startled at having his thoughts overheard. For the hundredth time he wished he had the Reader's training to decide when he wanted to be Read and when not, without having to concentrate on it.

He told Ashuru and Tadisha what Norgu had told him. "Djahat," said Ashuru. "That is much closer than Johara. Tadisha, Lord Lenardo knows you, but I fear to allow you to leave your body after what happened in the temple."

"And I fear," said Wulfston, "that Z'Nelia is keeping Lenardo unconscious. We know he can Read over five days' distance. If he hasn't contacted us, I do not think we can contact him."

"Then I must ask you again," said Ashuru, "will Lord Lenardo abide by a promise you give for him?"

"I believe he will," Wulfston replied, "if you will release him from it the moment your own healers can handle Z'Nelia."

"Agreed." Ashuru smiled, the first true smile of friendship she had given him. "I know you are concerned about your sister and the child she carries. If we succeed in our endeavor, you and Lord Lenardo should easily reach home in time for the birth of his daughter."

When Ashuru went to supervise the continuing preparation for war, Tadisha lingered beside Wulfston as they left their conference room. Karili and Warimu troops were arriving daily, and Norgu's castle overflowed with people. Structural repairs had been made quickly, as Z'Nelia's firestorm had not lasted long enough to destroy stone walls. New doors and window frames were already in place, and workmen pounded away with hammers as they replaced the wooden shakes on the roof of some areas. Where the roof was tiled, it might be blackened, but it remained sound.

There was a singular lack of furnishings, however; chairs, tables, and chests had gone up in flames, along with hangings, cushions, linens, and clothing. To Wulfston it was a sadly familiar situation. Fire was a favorite Adept weapon; he had spent many a day in similarly fire-stripped castles and villas.

He had hoped, he told Tadisha, that he had seen the last of such damage.

She shook her head sadly. "How can it ever end, except through some person of great powers eventually ruling all, destroying his enemies?"

"Is that what you would wish for?" he asked.

"No! No—the stories you tell of your lands, where Movers and Seers live together in peace . . . if only we could do the same."

They left the castle, Traylo and Arlus at their heels. The town was busy; they cut through a side street, out into what ought to be the countryside, but was now the camp-grounds of a growing army.

"Peace is possible—with vigilance," Wulfston said. "But it didn't happen in a day. We are still building trust among our people, and there are those along our borders who think us weaklings if we do not seek to conquer further. Every so often we have to fight off those who try to conquer us. Armies like this are not as common a sight as they once were in the Savage Empire, but there are still times when we must gather them."

"We," said Tadisha. "Us. I wonder if our Karili Assembly will ever have that kind of unity, when even among families we see such conflict. Z'Nelia, Chulaika, Norgu— deadly enemies despite being of one blood."

"One blood," Wulfston said flatly. "*My* blood."

An apology leaped to Tadisha's eyes. "I didn't—"

"I know." He smiled, silencing her with a gentle finger on her lips. "I needed to say it aloud. A part of me knew I would find such answers, long before I was forced to journey here and ask the questions. Even before Chulaika's ship entered the harbor in my land, that part of me was waiting for her . . . with dread. When she stood before my throne, I didn't need Seeing powers to know that she and I were related."

Tadisha stared at him. "How could you know? You said she was veiled, that all you could see were her eyes."

"Yes," he remembered, "her eyes. My memories of my mother are vague, but I remember her eyes. Deep, penetrating, sad—just like Chulaika's. Somehow I knew before I even reached Africa that Chulaika's hatred was toward blood kin."

He glanced at the dogs, who were playfully wrestling with each other, growling and barking. "It's why I named those two Traylo and Arlus, without recalling where the names came from. It was a story Nerius told Aradia and me, one time when we were fighting worse than usual.

"I was about twelve, and my powers were taking that leap at puberty that's also accompanied by lack of control. Father had determined that my powers were likely to become as great as his and Aradia's . . . and she resented it. At the time, I thought that was all she resented, but now I realize that Father was spending much more time with me than with Aradia."

"Kamas and I went through just such a situation not so long ago," said Tadisha.

"I suppose siblings always do," said Wulfston, "but your mother didn't let it get to the stage at which you did something unforgivable, any more than Nerius did. He separated Aradia and me—sent her off for a month with Lady Lilith, and me to an ally of his named Hron. Of course we discovered how much we missed each other, but when we came home the first thing Father did was to sit us down and tell us the story of Traylo and Arlus, brothers of equal powers who fought all their lives over who should hold power in their lands. In the end they killed each other. Nobody won, and their people were left leaderless."

"We also have such cautionary tales," said Tadisha.

"There are others," Wulfston agreed. "The reason the tale of Traylo and Arlus had such impact, though, is that it came with the object lesson—after being separated for a month, Aradia and I knew that we loved and missed one another and Nerius, and no power struggle was important enough to tear a family apart."

He thought for a moment, and then added, "Our alliance is like a family. Lenardo became family when he married Aradia. Julia became family when Lenardo adopted her." He turned to look at Tadisha. "I wish . . ."

But he could not complete the thought—it was the wrong time and place.

"I wish I could be a part of such a family," Tadisha completed it for him. "But that family is far away, and I have obligations here. Your family here—"

Wulfston shuddered. He still did not feel related to Norgu, Z'Nelia, Chulaika, or Chaiku, no matter what Barak said. "If you insist that blood will tell," he replied, "then you can never trust me. I couldn't trust myself if that were true!"

Tadisha grasped his hand. "Oh, no—I didn't intend— Wulfston, I only meant that you *have* family here, and thus responsibilities."

"I have responsibilities because I have given my word, not because I share some ancestors with the people who have attacked you. I will discharge those responsibilities, just as you will discharge yours, Princess of the Karili."

They looked into one another's eyes, they held hands, but they might as well have been standing on different continents. Her future lay here, in Africa, while his lay far across the sea, in the Savage Empire.

"If we defeat Z'Nelia," Tadisha murmured, "who will rule her lands? Norgu is not to be trusted, nor Chulaika, nor Chaiku if his mother raises him. Wulfston, you are of that family. Take the throne. The Karili Assembly will support you. Form an alliance here. Bring peace to Africa. We need you—"

"No, you don't," he told her firmly, easily identifying the strong temptation he felt as a desire to stay with Tadisha, not any rightful claim to the throne of the Zionae. "Your mother has already sown the seeds here with the Karili Assembly. I saw that Assembly stand up to Norgu. He will undoubtedly take Z'Nelia's throne; as her son he has a rightful claim to it. And you, your mother, your brother, and all the Movers and Seers of the Assembly will pool your strength to force him to use his powers for good . . . until it becomes a habit."

Reluctantly, he pushed Tadisha's hand aside, then turned and walked away from her toward where the troops were quartered who would be under his direct command in the battle to come.

Part of this army would be moving out in a few hours, and they were gathering supplies, packing wagons, and preparing tack for the ride.

Through the camp some boys pushed a cart with barrels of water from the town's wells, and men came forward to fill their water-bags.

Wulfston saw Zanos join the queue, his white skin and red hair a beacon even though his large frame was not unusual among the Warimu. He was glad to see the gladiator, and farther down the line the *Night Queen* crew members.

Zanos reached the head of the line. The boy turned the tap, and water poured into Zanos' water-bag until it was about half full; then he twisted off the flow.

"Fill it," Zanos said in broken Warimu. "I'm strong enough to carry it full."

Wulfston recognized that the water boy was Karili. He shook his head and said in his native language, "It can't be filled any further." Seeing that Zanos didn't understand, he tried Warimu with an accent even worse than the gladiator's. "I can't fill it further."

"Of course you can!" Zanos insisted. "Turn it on again!"

Wulfston half-saw, half-Read the mixture of annoyance and mischief in the water boy. He resented this strange white man trying to tell him his business, so he opened the tap again, more water tumbled into Zanos' bag—

The water-bag swelled, and then burst at the seams, drenching Zanos and rousing a hearty roar of laughter from the men behind him.

Zanos' face flushed with momentary fury, and he raised his arm as if to strike the boy. But before Wulfston had need to stop him he pulled his own punch, looked down at the limp water-bag, then up at the boy on the wagon, and burst into laughter.

Turning the threat into a clap on the buttocks that almost knocked the boy off the wagon, Zanos said, "You're right, boy! I should have listened to you. You go on doing your job right, no matter what anybody tells you!"

Wulfston recognized the skill of a man who had spent a lifetime performing in public, who dared not appear a poor sport. In fact, had he not been able to Read that the reaction was habit rather than feeling, he might have thought the old Zanos was returning. As it was, he sensed melancholy beneath the forced good cheer.

The *Night Queen* crew did not, however; they threw jeers and japes at Zanos, who fended them off with what appeared to be easy humor.

Zanos was obviously in control of himself. Wulfston decided not to approach him, and instead went on to inspect the troops assigned to his command.

These were not his people; he would command their

respect only *after* they had fought together. Wulfston found the officers had their men's respect, so he merely introduced himself, gave them a straightforward idea of what they could expect from his powers, and told them to follow their officers' orders.

When they moved out the next day, Ashuru told him, "Your troops are impressed with you."

"How could they be? They don't know me."

"Nor do you know them . . . and you know it. I gave you experienced warriors, and you wisely left them to the leaders they know. By showing your respect for them, you gained their respect, Lord Wulfston." She eyed him speculatively. "I do not know why it should surprise me anymore to find you a wise and skillful leader."

On the road, there was no chance for Wulfston and Tadisha to be alone—or at least none came naturally, and Tadisha showed no inclination to create such an opportunity. A few hours' ride from Djahat, Tadisha and Ashuru began to See ahead, Norgu, Kamas, and Wulfston letting the women's stronger powers focus on Z'Nelia's lands. Barak was told what they Saw.

The setting was almost identical to that in the Karili lands: a strong-walled castle surrounded by a city. But no armies gathered here; it appeared that Z'Nelia had left herself undefended.

"She has to know we're here," said Wulfston.

"Of course she does," agreed Ashuru. "She cannot think that a single Mover's powers can combat an army!"

"There are guards in the castle," Tadisha pointed out.

"Not enough to defend against us," said Norgu, "or against the Savishnon. She is so mad she thinks she can defeat our army and the Savishnon, all alone. But this time she has no volcano to unloose!"

Wulfston said, "I agree that she is mad, Norgu, but not in that way. Ashuru, Tadisha, can you See to the north-west of Djahat? Can Z'Nelia's armies be stationed there against the Savishnon?"

They did find some troops to the northwest, but still far too few for the oncoming threat.

Ashuru sighed. "We have no choice but to ride on. Norgu, keep your troops behind ours. Lord Wulfston, take Chulaika and Chaiku with you. You can resist Chulaika's attempts to use your powers."

They rode on, separate but united through Reading. As the hours passed, Wulfston felt himself grow more tense, the hair on the back of his neck prickling.

The road curved over the top of a hill, and Djahat appeared in the valley below. No army opposed them. No troops rushed to shut the city gates.

Wulfston looked out over the valley, the ancient and graceful city, the castle, the villages—

Villages? Dozens of villages so close to the city? There was not enough farmland here to support so many, and why house people in primitive huts when the city was right—

//It's a trap!// Wulfston exclaimed mentally. //Ashuru, Tadisha—focus on one of those villages!//

Sure enough, the cluster of huts was not a village at all, but merely empty shelters manned by armed troops!

//Spread out!// Ashuru broadcast.

//No!// Wulfston told her. //That's what Z'Nelia expects. She knows you are powerful Seers! She's got her troops scattered, expecting us to scatter ours to attack them. But Z'Nelia's *army* is not our goal!//

They understood at once.

Commands were broadcast mentally. Commands were shouted.

Their combined army rode straight down the hill and along the road toward Djahat.

They tore along the road at a gallop. Soldiers from the nearest huts ran to fend them off, but the Karili troops cut them down.

There was almost no Adept activity!

Spears and arrows were flung and deflected, but no

thunderbolts roared, no chasms opened at their horses' feet.

The gates of the city swung closed before they were halfway across the valley. For Wulfston it was child's play to set afire the wooden gates he could plainly see, sending the guards behind them scattering, hair and clothing singed.

Once the people were safe, he sent the intense fire of a funeral pyre, and the gates evaporated.

Wulfston lost track of Chulaika as the army galloped forward, right up the main street to the castle.

He did not ignite these gates, but added Adept force to the muscle power of the men and horses shoving against them as Z'Nelia's guards, outnumbered, tried to swing them closed. Sheer force triumphed, and they rode into the courtyard.

Wulfston jumped off his horse and ran up the steps to the entry, trying to Read inside. //*Lenardo?*//

//*Wulfston?*// The mental reply was weak, but his brother was alive and conscious.

Tadisha fought her way into the courtyard and joined Wulfston.

Zanos, Telek, and the rest of the *Night Queen* crew struggled with the guards at the gates.

"Keep them open till Ashuru gets in!" Wulfston shouted. "And Kamas and Barak!" He turned to Tadisha. "Where's Norgu?"

"He held his armies back," she replied, letting him See with her. Then, "Wulfston!"

From the northwest, where they had been waiting just outside of normal Seeing range, the Savishnon hordes swept toward Djahat!

Norgu and his troops would be caught on the open highway, the Savishnon attacking from the west, Z'Nelia's army from the east!

"I hope Norgu uses his powers wisely!" was all Wulfston could offer.

Ashuru was inside the courtyard now, herding Chulaika

before her. Kamas pushed his way through to make a path for Barak, then shielded the old man as he helped him down from his horse.

"Close those gates!" Wulfston shouted.

"Our army—" Tadisha protested.

"No army can help us in here, but they might be used against us. Tadisha, See inside. Lenardo's alive, but there's something wrong with his Reading. Where's Z'Nelia?"

Tadisha had no need to answer. A thunderbolt shattered the air, and only Wulfston's instincts snatched her out of the way of death.

He couldn't Read Z'Nelia because she was braced to use her Mover's powers, of course.

"Read for Lenardo!" he told Tadisha. "I'll protect you.

"I can't— Wait—he's in the tower. Come on!"

Tadisha ran inside. Wulfston followed, Ashuru hard on his heels, dragging Chulaika. Kamas swept up Chaiku and followed, Barak trailing.

Suddenly the walls and floor were afire! Heat blazed from all sides; smoke suffocated them.

Wulfston turned his powers to putting out the fire—and couldn't! It blazed on, choking them.

Coughing, eyes watering, he fell to his knees, mustering all his force to beat back the flames—

"Lord Wulfston, no!"

Barak stooped beside him, grasping his arm. "It is a vision, not real! Z'Nelia is making you waste your powers."

He couldn't breathe. And yet . . . nothing was consumed. The flames licked at their clothing, but it did not catch fire. Their skin burned painfully, but it did not blister.

"Ignore it!" Wulfston choked out. "Come on." And he started forward again.

They stumbled through the blazing corridor into a connecting hall, where the conflagration ended. The moment they stepped into the clear air, guards charged them with spears.

Veteran of many Adept battles, Wulfston knew he had to conserve his powers. It might have been impressive to stop the spears, perhaps even turn them in midair. But it was more practical to stop the throwers. A mental tug at the knees, and a man dropped in a heap.

Kamas Saw, laughed, and invoked his limited Mover's powers to do the same to two more.

But others emerged all along the hallway, too many to take one at a time.

Ashuru sidestepped a spear and caught it in a neat combination of physical strength and limited Mover's power. She turned and flung it at the astonished man who had thrown it—a deathblow.

More guards came, seemingly out of nowhere, determined to fight to the death. Knocking a man down meant only that he bounced up again, grabbed any fallen weapon, and came at them once more.

Wulfston sent many into Adept sleep, but even that use of his power was draining. There were too many!

In the crowded corridor, the battle was both physical and mental. Wulfston could not stop to Read. He struck at what he saw.

Three men charged him. He put one into Adept sleep, stopped the second one's heart, but as he was turning to the third, a spear caught the man in the gut, and he doubled over with a scream of agony.

Tadisha stepped from behind Wulfston, pulled the spear from the slowly dying man, and drove it mercifully through his throat.

Even as she took the time to grant a swift death, another guard was on her, knife raised.

Wulfston dropped him in his tracks with hardly a thought, just as rough hands grabbed him from behind.

He lost sight of Tadisha as he went down in a heap of bodies on the bloody floor. But when he fought his way out he heard yells of triumph from the direction of the courtyard.

Zanos and Telek had found them.

Fighting as if they were partners rather than rivals, the two huge white men flung Zionae guards right and left, dealing death as casually as they might pick apples.

Z'Nelia's guards scattered before them—but only for a moment.

It seemed as if hundreds more poured into the corridor, blocking their way as they struggled toward the entry to the tower. Chulaika had somehow reached the bottom of the steps, where she cowered, holding Chaiku before her.

"The gates?" Wulfston panted to Zanos when the two came together in the melee.

"They'll hold!" the gladiator assured him, punching a man's face inward to a crunch of mangled flesh no longer horrifying in that corridor of death.

On they fought, working step by slow step toward the tower stairs, until at last no more guards appeared and they stood gasping, blood-covered, but alive.

Tadisha was limping.

Barak leaned on a spear to steady his steps, but he was only exhausted, not injured.

Kamas cradled a broken arm.

Ashuru had a cut on her cheek and a blackening eye.

Chulaika held Chaiku, his face hidden against his mother's shoulder.

Zanos and Telek showed numerous scratches and bruises, but no serious injuries.

"Kamas," said Wulfston, "I must set your arm."

"Don't put me to sleep!" the boy said.

"I won't," he assured him. "Tadisha, Ashuru, See what's happening. We don't want another surprise attack."

Kamas gritted his teeth as Wulfston pulled the bone ends back together, then invoked the healing fire to knit them. It would take a day of healing sleep to knit completely, but for the time being Kamas would not damage it merely by moving around.

"The gates are still closed," Ashuru reported. "Except

for the dead, there is no one but us in the castle . . . and Z'Nelia waits for us in the tower."

They climbed the stairs.

The door to the tower room swung open as they approached.

Lenardo was standing by the window, looking pale and drawn. But he was alive!

Wulfston took a step toward him, crying his name. Z'Nelia stepped out of nowhere, into his path.

Chulaika's features. His mother's eyes . . . burning with madness!

"Welcome, Beast Lord!" she said.

Suddenly his every nerve was aflame with pure pain!

Wulfston screamed, vaguely aware of the screams of his companions.

"Wulfston!"

Lenardo's voice.

"Wulfston, open to Reading!" the Master Reader gasped.

Their minds met—and although Lenardo did not have his usual power, he showed them that the pain was not real. Had Z'Nelia actually seared their nerves, they would be dead.

As the Seers' minds joined, the pain eased. Even Barak and Telek broke free.

Z'Nelia cried, "Seers you may be, but I am the greatest Mover of all!"

This time she caused real damage!

With no defenses, Telek fell dead.

Wulfston fought, felt Zanos' powers joined to his, and Lenardo's Adept power, small though it was—

"Tadisha! Ashuru! Kamas! Join your Movers' powers to mine!" he cried.

They did, but against Z'Nelia's strength, hoarded while they fought their way through her guards, their power was insufficient.

Z'Nelia's mad laughter floated around them. Wulfston gripped Lenardo's hand on one side, Tadisha's on the

other. Ashuru grasped Tadisha's other hand, and the rest
joined the circle until Chulaika stood alone with Chaiku,
Barak and Kamas reaching toward her—

She thrust her son into the circle and closed it.

Renewed strength flowed around the circle until thunderbolts rained on them, too many to deflect—

Looking across the circle at Zanos, feeling the man's
desperate fury at being defeated in his revenge on the
woman who had murdered his wife, Wulfston suddenly
remembered Zanos and the burst water bag.

The scene seemed significant—but why?

Then he knew.

"Stop fighting her! *Support her!*" he gasped through
pain. "Feed . . . energy back to her! Flood her!"

Ashuru stared, but she and Tadisha together joined
their strength to Wulfston's, directing their energy to
Z'Nelia as if it were healing power. Lenardo joined them
at once, giving what little strength he had. Kamas did his
part, and Barak stood transfixed, maintaining the circle.

Z'Nelia drank in the energy. Their pain diminished as
she greedily soaked up the pure power.

Wulfston urged more on her, and his plan began to take
effect!

From reveling, Z'Nelia's feelings turned to faint discomfort, confusion—and then fear as more energy flowed into
her!

Chulaika realized what was happening, as did Zanos,
and they added their force, Chulaika focusing Chaiku's
power on her twin sister.

The Zionae queen's nerves seared, her own energy
overflowing her control. They broke the circle, reformed
it around her, preventing her from casting the energy
away.

Z'Nelia fell to her knees, keening in agony. Chaiku
stared at her, then up at his mother, terrified to find his
mother's face on this stranger.

The witch-queen's pain and terror grew. She fell, her body twitching grotesquely.

"Don't kill her!" Wulfston exclaimed. "We've won. Lenardo—Ashuru—?"

It was Ashuru who replied, "She is helpless. There is no need to kill her."

Ashuru had stopped pouring forth energy to See Z'Nelia. Lenardo was too weak to do more; Wulfston, Tadisha, and Kamas stopped together—

"No!" screamed Zanos. "She must die!"

Zanos and Chulaika refused to stop!

Wulfston turned, intending to knock them unconscious with his greater powers, when the stink of burning flesh filled the small room, and Z'Nelia's death-screech shocked through their already-battered nerves.

In the white-hot fire of a funeral pyre, Z'Nelia's body was consumed.

There was silence. Lenardo slumped to the floor.

Wulfston turned on Zanos. "Why?" he demanded.

"She killed Astra," the gladiator replied. "She had to die."

"And now this land will be torn apart—" Wulfston began, when suddenly a scream erupted behind him. He turned, saw Chulaika on the floor, writhing—

He opened to Reading, and with the Seers observed the unimaginable.

Z'Nelia's spirit was fighting for possession of her twin sister's body!

Chapter Eight

*H*elplessly, the Seers observed as Z'Nelia fought for possession of Chulaika's body. Equal in determination, neither would give way—until the body, weakened by the long struggle, collapsed.

Chaiku wailed, trying to wake his mother, until Ashuru bent and picked him up, cuddling him with a mother's instinct while her mind still probed Chulaika's.

Wulfston Read with them, his own Reading powers barely maintaining the link after he had poured out his Adept energy. He could feel Lenardo, too, only tenuously keeping touch, letting Ashuru and Tadisha search the mind of the woman on the floor, to find out which sister had survived.

Only to discover . . . both.

Two minds seethed angrily within the one person, but with the body they inhabited unconscious, it appeared that they must wait in frustration for its awakening to continue their contest.

The Seers withdrew, leaving Chulaika unconscious.

Wulfston looked around. The room was small, with a narrow window. No sounds of battle came through it.

A heap of ashes marked Z'Nelia's physical remains. Telek's body lay near the door. Wulfston looked for Zanos, wanting to make the man understand what he had done, but the gladiator had gone.

Lenardo sat cross-legged on the floor, struggling not to faint from weakness. Wulfston knelt beside him, lending strength from the last of his reserves. Lenardo looked up gratefully, but as soon as the desire to lapse into unconsciousness passed he put his hand on Wulfston's arm, shaking his head. "Save your strength. There may be other healing to do."

Wulfston looked up sharply at Tadisha. Her eyes took on a faraway look. "The battle is over," she said. "Z'Nelia's army was divided. The Savishnon overran the western troops, but were weakened enough that our combined armies defeated them, and have taken the city. Our Healers are already working among the wounded. It appears that we may safely take the time to heal ourselves."

"Norgu?" Wulfston asked.

"Unharmed except for the weakness after battle."

"Thank Shangonu for that!" added Ashuru. "If that boy had the strength left, he would grasp this chance to seize the throne."

"He will certainly try soon," agreed Tadisha.

"Z'Nelia will fight him," said Lenardo, "unless we can drive her from her sister's body."

"Will you help us do that, Master Reader?" asked Ashuru.

Lenardo gave a grim smile. "In my present condition I don't know how much help I can be, but you will certainly have all I can give, Queen Ashuru."

Wulfston thought belatedly of introductions, and then realizd that none were necessary between Readers and Seers.

They lifted Chulaika's body onto the narrow bed in this room where Z'Nelia had kept Lenardo, and dragged Telek's body out onto the landing. Uninjured soldiers were in the castle now, carrying out the dead.

The charnelhouse of the corridor where they had fought Z'Nelia's guards lay in their path. They had no choice except to go through it, and out into the blood-smeared courtyard, where the bodies had already been removed.

The servants' wing of the castle, though, had not been touched. Karili had taken over the kitchen, and were sorting through the supplies to put a meal together for those who had exerted Adept powers.

Wulfston's stomach was giving him conflicting signals: he was "hungry as a Mover," and yet sick at what he had just been through. Someone handed him a flagon of fresh milk, and he drank it gratefully as their little group proceeded into a room furnished with worn but luxurious carpets and cushions, where Ashuru and Tadisha's serving-women were waiting to remove their blood-spattered outer garments, providing clean caftans for all.

Finally Wulfston asked Lenardo, "What happened to you? I've been worried ever since Z'Nelia took you from Norgu, and you didn't contact me."

"I couldn't," Lenardo replied, taking a piece of fruit from a tray servants had already brought in. Wulfston noticed for the first time how thin and gaunt Lenardo looked. "Every minute I've been awake, I've had to fight Z'Nelia. Whenever her attention was called elsewhere, she put me into Adept sleep."

"And didn't bother to feed you," Wulfston noted.

"Not often," Lenardo agreed. "She wanted me weak; she kept probing my mind, sifting through my memories. I don't know what she wanted, Wulfston, but I gave her as little as possible. I assume she wasn't satisfied, because she never gave up—even today, when she knew you were approaching from one direction, the Savishnon from another." He shook his head with a smile. "Thank the gods you finally got here! I've never been so glad to see you in my life!"

Lenardo reached out to squeeze Wulfston's hand, an unusual gesture from a Reader. Wulfston gripped the thin hand in return, reassured that Lenardo really was well and needed only rest and food to be his old self.

"You'll want this," he said, removing Lenardo's ring from his finger and handing it to his sister's husband.

Lenardo smiled. "Thank you for keeping it safe for me. Aradia would never forgive me if I lost it." He slipped it onto his finger, and turned it, studying the entwined emblems of wolf and dragon. "Did you send another message to Aradia?" he asked.

"Yes, with one of Ashuru's people. Now you can write her a letter."

"We should be home before any letter," said Lenardo.

"Doesn't that depend on how long it takes to drive Z'Nelia out of Chulaika's body?"

The Master Reader nodded. "However, if we cannot do it soon, I fear it will be Chulaika who is driven out by Z'Nelia."

Wulfston shuddered. "I hope not. But if that should happen . . . I made a promise to Ashuru in return for the help of the Karili in rescuing you: that you would help her to restore Z'Nelia to sanity."

"All I want to do is go home," said Lenardo, "but I will honor the promise you made in my name . . . if it should prove necessary."

From across the room, Tadisha was watching Wulfston and Lenardo. Servants brought cooked food, placing it on clean woven mats on the floor. She turned to aid Kamas, whose broken arm still pained him.

Lenardo ate meat without protest, although he always claimed it blurred his Reading powers. Right now he needed to restore his physical strength.

Norgu joined them, warily accepting their congratulations on the victory against the Savishnon. The boy was closed tightly against Reading. Wulfston feared that he thought they had tricked him into remaining behind the main army, hoping he would be killed. By silent consent they told him only that Z'Nelia was dead. Perhaps tomorrow they would be able to drive her from Chulaika's body, and have only Norgu to worry about.

There was little conversation, as everyone was bone-weary. Reports came in all through the meal of areas secured. More troops from other members of the Karili Assembly were approaching; by morning they would drive another wedge between Djahat and the Savishnon, forcing them even farther back and leaving the Seers and Lenardo free to work with Chulaika.

It was almost noon before Wulfston woke the next day, much restored. The smell of food guided him downstairs, to find Lenardo, Tadisha, and Ashuru being served in the same room where they had gathered yesterday.

"Norgu has gone to join his army to the others," Ashuru reported. "This is a good time to attempt to drive Z'Nelia out."

Wulfston nodded. "Shall I stand guard?"

"No," relied Lenardo. "I want your strength in the rapport, Wulfston."

"In the—? Lenardo, I'm no Master Reader!"

"And I'm no Lord Adept. You understand the way a Mover's mind works as neither Ashuru nor I can. And you can provide an anchor for us. Ashuru and I will be out of body. You will Read with us, and guide us back should Z'Nelia attempt to lose us on the planes of existence."

"Is that what happened to the Seers who tried to See into the Dead Lands?" he asked.

"Apparently," said Ashuru. "This is something our Seers could learn from your Master Readers. We have little experience wiht these 'planes of existence,' for many who have attempted to explore them have either been lost, or returned as mad as Z'Nelia."

Lenardo nodded. "So did many Readers who first attempted to reach them, but eventually we developed safeguards, and now we can often cure minds which have been influenced by communication with those planes which we do not understand." He shook his head. "I do not know what we will encounter in driving Z'Nelia out of Chulaika, but I have relied on Wulfston's strength many times before. I trust him."

Tadisha asked, "What do you want me to do, Lord Lenardo?"

The Master Reader looked toward Ashuru. "I do not

know what experience your daughter has had, Queen Ashuru. By our standards at home, she would probably qualify as a Magister Reader. If I were her teacher at Gaeta, if she had already had experience in healing sick minds I would want her to have this opportunity despite the danger. But this should be no one's first experience of mental healing."

Ashuru nodded. "As a mother, I would protect her. As a teacher, though, I believe she is ready to participate."

"Very well, then. We can begin."

Barak had gone out to observe the battle, and Kamas was still in healing sleep. So it was Lenardo, Ashuru, Tadisha, and Wulfston who went to the tower room where Chulaika slept, her body containing Z'Nelia's presence as well as her own.

Not allowing the woman's body to waken, they reached out to the two minds.

//Chaiku!// Chulaika demanded. //Where is my son?//

//Well cared for,// Ashuru told her. //Do not worry; you will soon hold him in your arms again.//

//*Never* again!// Z'Nelia raged. //*I* will hold him! *I* will raise him, teach him *my* ways. Leave me, Chulaika. You have lost this battle.//

//No, Z'Nelia,// Lenardo told her, //this time you have lost. You have no right to Chulaika's body. Accept your death, and go in peace to the plane of the dead.//

//You think you can kill me again?// Z'Nelia demanded. //I will kill you all!//

Without warning, they were no longer in the tower room of the castle in Djahat, but on the lip of the crater on Mount Manjuro!

Heat pulled the sweat through their pores. The ground beneath their feet trembled as the lava heaved. The sky was black with ash and smoke. The only light was the lurid red-orange glare of the lava, reflecting off two figures locked in mortal struggle: Z'Nelia and Chulaika, each trying to thrust the other into the bubbling lava.

But as they fought, glancing down into the heaving pit, inside the crater was no longer lava, but a seething maelstrom of malice, anger, rage, lust, jealousy, guilt—

Wulfston slowly regained self-awareness, and realized that it was Lenardo interpreting the imagery, letting them all understand what the magma represented to Z'Nelia and Chulaika. And something else. He could sense the Master Reader trying to identify some sensation that remained frustratingly just out of reach.

The moment Wulfston found himself, the other Seers were "there," standing on the brink of the lake of chaos, watching the twin forms struggling on the opposite side.

Lenardo staggered, and Wulfston grasped his arm to keep him from falling. "What—?"

But there was no need to speak. The moment he thought of the question, he knew the answer: Z'Nelia had created this mind-world, and so it operated by the rules she had laid down for it. She had decided that the physical strength of each person within this world would depend on the strength of that person's talents at the moment he entered it. And Lenardo's talents had been weakened by her mistreatment.

"She fears you," Wulfston told Lenardo, willingly supporting the Master Reader.

"And from her fear of me," Lenardo observed, "she has created her own destruction."

For, it seemed, her death trauma had weakened Z'Nelia's own talents so that she had no more power than Chulaika. It was an evenly matched battle!

Tadisha, though, was fully recovered. Young and strong, she began to run lightly along the rim of the volcano.

"Tadisha, no!" Wulfston called.

"Go with her!" said Lenardo, sinking cross-legged to the ground. "I am safe here."

"Go with Tadisha," agreed Ashuru, starting around the lip of the volcano in the opposite direction.

Not quite sure what they would do when they reached

the battling twins—tear them apart? throw Z'Nelia into the volcano?—Wulfston and Tadisha nonetheless fought their way across the treacherous ground, against a rising wind. On the other side, Ashuru's figure grew dim as the crater spewed up drifts of chaos, threatening to overflow and engulf them all.

The forms of Z'Nelia and Chulaika became clearer as they approached. What should they do?

Suddenly, behind the battling women a new figure appeared!

It was a man, young and strong, slender and muscular, brandishing a diamond-tipped spear.

Norgu!

Norgu not as he was, but his ideal image of himself as a grown man, which—by Z'Nelia's own rules—he could maintain here because he was in full possession of his powers!

Norgu strode toward the struggling women, spear at the ready.

Wulfston and Tadisha ran against the wind which tore the words from their mouths and tossed them away as they shouted at him to stop—

—too late!

With the point of his spear, he caught Z'Nelia in the small of the back as she strove to push Chulaika into the pit.

The spear shoved Z'Nelia against Chulaika, and both women tumbled into the maelstrom, locked together, screaming with one voice as Norgu howled with triumphant laughter!

Wulfston leaped toward him. Norgu spun, aiming the spear at him. "You die, too, Beast Lord!"

Ashuru arrived behind him. "Stop, Norgu!"

Norgu turned to her. "Ah, the Queen of the Karili. How convenient. I shall rid myself of all my enemies at once, and rule Africa uncontested!"

Norgu drew back the spear as if to thrust it into Ashuru. Tadisha cried, "Mother!" and tried to grasp Norgu's arm.

He sidestepped her, swinging the spear toward Tadisha now, its diamond tip about to gut her.

Wulfston dived for the shaft, hauling the tip down short of its mark. He rolled, wrenching the spear from Norgu's hands, unable to stop as his momentum carried him toward the lip of the crater!

Chaos rushed up at him, delirium and madness reaching out to envelop him—

With every vestige of strength he could command, he flung the spear ahead of him, the momentum shoving him backwards at the very edge so that he stopped with his hands on the lip of the crater, his head hanging over, peering into the pit as it erupted!

The volcano of greed, guilt, jealousy, and power-hunger belched out its core of madness.

Tadisha on one side and Ashuru on the other grasped Wulfston's arms, hauling him to his feet. As they started back toward where they had left Lenardo, Ashuru shouted, "Norgu! Come with us!"

But as they rounded the rim to where they could see him without having to turn around, they found that Norgu hadn't followed.

The fountain of chaos tossed the diamond-headed spear tantalizingly out of Norgu's reach. The boy tried to grasp it.

"Let it go!" shouted Wulfston, but Norgu paid no heed.

The fiery plume shifted. The spear fell down into the chasm. Magma erupted; Norgu was engulfed where he stood, his screams drowned in the roar.

The soil beneath them heaved.

They stumbled on toward Lenardo.

Smoke blinded them. Heat blistered their skin.

A wave of chaos washed over them, tearing them apart!

"Lenardo!" Wulfston shouted, lost in a storm of fury. Only the Master Reader could get them home. But where was he? "Lenardo! Lenarrrdddooo!"

He tried to Read, couldn't, remembered that he *was* Reading this whole scene—

*   *   *

Wulfston hurt. He was aware of aching in every muscle and bone before he felt the finger pressed firmly to his forehead between the eyes, and heard Lenardo's voice saying calmly, "Wulfston, wake up. It's all over. Wake up now."

He did, with a moan.

He was slumped on his side, cheek against the cold stone floor, legs twisted painfully. He had fallen sideways from the cross-legged position he had assumed to Read with the others. The more awake he became, the more agony assaulted his nerves. Nothing that happened in Adept battle had ever hurt this much!

Light stabbed his eyes when he opened them to find a blurry Lenardo bending over him. "I know it hurts," the Master Reader said, "but you'll be all right. You weren't prepared to go out of body."

"Is that what I did?" he managed to get out. Even his tongue hurt.

"Yes. Don't try to move. Can you start healing yourself?"

He found that he could. Relief and warmth spread through his cold, cramped limbs. Lenardo gently straightened his body, massaging the abused muscles. "What happened?" Wulfston asked. "I shouldn't have fallen."

"I know; the worst that should have happened from leaving your body in that position is a few cramped muscles. Norgu may have shoved your body over out of spite, when he discovered what we were doing."

Healing, Wulfston could not Read. "Tadisha? Ashuru?"

"They're fine. They've gone to find Norgu."

"Or his body," Wulfston said bitterly.

"Not necessarily," Lenardo told him. "Chulaika's still alive."

"Did we . . . drive out Z'Nelia?"

"I'm not sure. She's in a coma, and I'm not ready right now to Read her that deeply."

That had to wait for the next day. Today they healed

themselves once more. Lenardo and Wulfston ate, then went to their own rooms to sleep. They rested comfortably, for the news from the battlefield was good: the Karili allies had sent the Savishnon into retreat once again, and if the followers of the war god could never be persuaded to change their ways, at least their numbers had been decimated. There would be a few years of peace.

But under whose rule?

In the morning, Wulfston found that their problems were far from resolved.

Norgu was no longer an immediate threat. Tadisha, Ashuru, and Barak escorted back to the castle a living, unharmed body . . . with a mind that seemed to comprehend less than Chaiku's.

The trauma Norgu had suffered when his mother took her revenge at the dream-volcano had erased his knowledge and memories, leaving him a hulking, helpless infant. Ashuru and Lenardo found no injury to his intelligence; he began immediately relearning, and within a few days could already babble a few words. He was still completely self-centered, but it was normal for his apparent stage of infancy. Perhaps this time, if he grew up under the proper supervision, he would mature in character as well as intelligence and powers.

Chulaika was another matter. Lenardo and Ashuru spent hours beside her comatose body, trying to reach her mind. Eventually they discovered something quite unexpected.

"It's as if Z'Nelia and Chulaika are uniting to form one individual!" Ashuru explained.

"When Norgu thrust them together into that maelstrom of destruction," Lenardo speculated, "they were forced to depend on each other, or they would have been as devastated by it as he was."

"Do you think they can integrate?" Wulfston asked. "Can you help them?"

"We're trying," said Ashuru. "Only time will tell if a person capable of ruling the Zionae will emerge."

But time was something they did not have. Neither the Zionae nor the Warimu had a leader. If they did not settle those people's fears soon, some of them would try to assume leadership, creating civil war.

Lenardo gave Wulfston a grim smile. "You know what you have to do. You and Aradia taught me, remember?"

Aradia had tested Lenardo's mettle by throwing him to the wolves—giving him a conquered land to rule, alone. And the Lord Reader had succeeded far beyond Wulfston's expectations. He had never discovered whether it had been beyond Aradia's.

Much as it disturbed him, Wulfston recognized that Lenardo was right: someone had to take command, and Wulfston was the logical candidate.

The Zionae and the Warimu were accustomed to being ruled by strength. Only a powerful leader could unite them to the Karili Assembly. And with Z'Nelia/Chulaika in coma and Norgu reduced to mental infancy, Wulfston was the only leader available with the Mover's powers they respected.

So, before any minor leader decided to make his move, Ashuru called the Karili Assembly into session in the audience chamber of the palace of Djahat. But she did not take the throne; rather, she took center place in the Assembly, who faced the throne as visiting dignitaries.

The officers of the Zionae and Warimu armies were also the chieftains of their towns and villages. Wulfston invited them into the audience chamber. When all were assembled, he made his entrance, dressed in the richest garments they could find in the palace, including a golden crown. Lenardo walked beside him, similarly attired. Thus they declared themselves the equals of the kings of the African nations.

Wulfston took the throne, to a mutter of astonishment. Lenardo stood at his side. Neither man was armed, nor was Barak, who stepped forward to flank Wulfston on the opposite side.

Wulfston waited until the whispers died into hushed expectancy. "Most of you do not know me," he said, "but you know who I am: Lord Wulfston of the Savage Empire. This is Lord Lenardo, Master Reader—the greatest Seer among our people. He is also my brother—my sister's husband—and the reason I am in Africa.

"When Lenardo was kidnapped and brought to Africa, I was forced to come here, and became involved in your wars with one another and the Zionae. Here I discovered that I am Zionae. My ancestors built this palace, and ruled these very lands.

"My grandmother was Katalia, who was murdered by her nephew Desak, the father of Z'Nelia and Chulaika. I am their cousin, and Norgu's one generation removed. Z'Nelia is dead, and her sister Chulaika is in coma. Norgu is incapacitated, and Chulaika's son Chaiku is only three years old.

"Therefor, by right of blood and conquest, I am now the ruler of these lands."

In the silent, sullen hush, Barak stepped forward. "I Verify what Lord Wulfston has told you of his ancestry, by my Grioka's powers."

People looked at one another uneasily. To most of them, Wulfston was an unknown quantity.

One of the Warimu chiefs stepped forward. "Are you not the Lord of the Black Wolf, reports of whose conquests have come to us from the lands across the Northern Sea?"

"I am," Wulfston agreed, squashing his feelings of irony that at last that song was doing him some positive good in Africa.

"You led the assault on the castle," said one of the Zionae officers. "Your Mover's powers destroyed more than a hundred of our best men."

"If Z'Nelia had not captured Lenardo, I would have had no reason to enter the castle," Wulfston reminded him.

"Nor," he added, sensing that he had their attention and

growing respect, "do I want to rule the lands of the Zionae or the Warimu."

There was a murmur of disbelief. Wulfston let it fade before he continued. "I have lands and peoples of my own, to whom I have responsibilities. I cannot stay in Africa. However, I have incurred obligations here by my actions, and discovered obligations of kinship. Therefor, I appoint as my regent in Africa Queen Ashuru of the Karili."

All eyes turned to the Karili queen, who stood wrapped in dignity, waiting for the protest to be voiced.

It was. "Ashuru is a Seer, not a Mover," the Zionae officer pointed out. "She has no powers with which to battle our enemies."

"Powers do not make great leaders," Wulfston replied. "The greatest enemy you have faced is the Savishnon. Z'Nelia defeated them with her Mover's powers, but almost destroyed herself in the process. And all that happened was that the Savishnon regrouped and came back four years later.

"You were all in the most recent battle. How were the Savishnon defeated this time? Not by Movers' powers, but by you, the combined armies of the Zionae, the Warimu, the Karili, and the members of the Assembly.

"*There* is your secret of peace and safety," Wulfston explained. "It lies in unity, in alliances between peaceful nations, standing together against those who spend their energies in mindless conquest.

"The Karili Assembly drove the Savishnon from their lands by uniting in a common cause. Queen Ashuru brought them together, and has led them successfully through this test of their union. I trust her as my regent, and you will soon grow to trust her when you prosper under her rule."

He did not mention the problem of Chulaika/Z'Nelia. Chulaika's body still lay in coma, both sisters' mental presences within it, slowly integrating as if they might eventually become one person.

Lenardo kept his agreement to help Ashuru. Each day

they spent hours in rapport with the twin minds, attempting to help them integrate.

Wulfston spent the time at first in a futile attempt to arrange a peace conference with the Savishnon leaders. They would not even discuss it. Savishna, he learned, mandated war and conquest until the whole world was under the rule of the war god, at which time the world would end and all who had fought gloriously in the cause would be united with Savishna for an eternity of celebration.

Followers of the weak, peaceful Shangonu, he was told, would be destroyed.

There was no foundation on which to make a truce, let alone a lasting peace. The Savishnon would lick their wounds, regroup, and attack again. And they would probably continue to do so until the last one of them died.

It was incomprehensible to him how anyone could think as the Savishnon did, so in the end he could only console himself with the idea that strengthening the Karili Assembly meant that the Savishnon would have enough to occupy them in Africa for the next few generations, and would not set out across the sea to attack his friends or his descendants.

Thinking of descendants, though, always brought his thoughts to Tadisha. Some days she worked with her mother and Lenardo, attempting to integrate Z'Nelia and Chulaika, but on others she stood as her mother's representative, reminding Wulfston that she would be Queen of the Karili one day, and that meant she would live out her life in Africa.

He didn't want Tadisha to stay in Africa; he wanted to take her home as his wife.

And she wanted him to stay here and rule.

Both were impossible.

Still, they could not resist having what time they could together. One evening they stood on the parapets, watching the sun set in red and gold splendor. Tadisha had worked with Lenardo and Ashuru that day, and was mentally but not physically tired.

"Lord Lenardo is teaching me so much," she said. "But it is frustrating."

"How so?"

"Z'Nelia resists the final integration with Chulaika. Yet once that is achieved, Lenardo's obligation will be fulfilled, and you and he will leave."

Wulfston had no answer to that. It was true.

Tadisha was silent for a moment, then said, "I once hoped to persuade you to stay with me."

"I know."

"Do you know when I knew it was impossible?" she asked.

"No."

"When we rescued Lenardo. He was so weak after Z'Nelia's torture—we might as well put the right name to what she did to him. I have seen it in his mind, things he would not tell you . . . but I think you knew anyway."

"I know Lenardo," he replied.

"Yes," she said softly, "just as I knew when Kamas was trying to hide the pain of his broken arm. That was when I Saw it, Wulfston. Lenardo is as much your brother as Kamas is mine. You had told me that your ties were to your family in the Savage Empire, but the first time I saw you and Lenardo together was the first time I understood in my heart that your bonds of love are as strong as bonds of blood."

"Tadisha," he said gently, "you must know how that can be. Every true marriage is such a bond of love. Every adoption of a child," he added, thinking of the way Chaiku had taken to Ashuru. "You may have a new little brother if you cannot bring Chulaika out of her coma, or if she recovers, but cannot care for Chaiku."

'I know," said Tadisha. "But I already have a brother who is almost a grown man. Kamas proved himself in battle and now he stands in for Mother on the days I am in the rapport."

She was closed against Reading. Wulfston looked into

her face in the fading light, trying to tell if she was offering him hope. He was afraid to take it, afraid to expose his heart to the disappointment of mistaking her meaning.

"Your mother once said you could learn a great deal from our Master Readers," he suggested.

She turned toward him with a smile. "Yes. And what would be better for the Karili than an alliance with the famous Lord of the Black Wolf?"

"Tadisha!" At last he dared to take her in his arms, to kiss her, to hold her close. He needed the reality of her slender form against him to believe it was possible—

"Wulfston?" she whispered against his cheek.

"Yes?"

"Will you marry me?"

He laughed. "I will if you will marry me!" he told her. "You will be welcome in my lands, Tadisha. And, although the journey is long, you will see your home again, and surely your family will visit us."

She hugged him tightly. "I think Mother knows, but I will go now and tell her officially." Then she slipped from his arms and was gone, leaving him breathless in the cool night air, fearing that Ashuru might forbid it, knowing that she had no reason except to lose her only daughter to the lord of a far-distant land.

Ashuru did not leave him in trepidation for long. By the time he descended the tower stairs, a servant was there to request that he attend the Karili queen in her chambers.

He felt once more that he faced the lion in her den.

Ashuru was seated, flanked by Tadisha and Kamas, all three closed to Reading. "Lord of the Black Wolf, you ask for my daughter in marriage?"

"I do," he replied, "and offer the Karili nation both the assurance of support in time of need, and trade in time of prosperity. Like you, Queen Ashuru, I speak for several nations joined in an alliance. I can offer your Seers the knowledge of our Master Readers. You may send your Seers to train in our Academies, and we will send our Readers to share their knowledge, and learn from you."

She waved that aside. "But what do you offer my daughter?"

"My hand, my throne . . . my heart," he replied simply.

"Tadisha, will you then renounce your claims as my heir to your brother Kamas?"

"Yes, Mother, gladly," Tadisha replied.

"Very well," Ashuru replied, still the majestic lioness. "Lord Wulfston, you arrived in our lands with nothing, and have proved yourself a valuable ally. Lord Lenardo has shown me how much our Seers could learn from your Readers. A union with your Savage Empire will provide us with much of value. And I believe that despite your lineage, you can be trusted to treat my daughter with love and respect."

"I promise that, Queen Ashuru."

"However," she continued, "I must make one condition: you must fulfill an obligation of blood."

"An . . . obligation of blood?"

"Your cousin Norgu."

"Norgu? What about him?"

"Lord Lenardo believes that the Master Readers in your Savage Empire could help Norgu to regain his mental capacities. But along with his mental growth, his great powers as a Mover will return. If he does not have the right guidance, he will grow again into the dangerous, spiteful, selfish man we saw here. A Seer cannot discipline a Mover of such strength. Norgu must be raised by a powerful Mover—a man like his father who might have turned him into a true leader. But Matu's death left no one with both the power and the wisdom to teach Norgu. You saw the result."

"I saw it," Wulfston replied, his mouth dry. She couldn't mean . . . ?

She did.

"The condition I place upon your marriage to Tadisha is that you take Norgu as your ward. You are a Lord Adept, a powerful Mover with the strength to control him. You control your powers; you do not let them control you. Teach this to Norgu, Lord Wulfston. Bring him to manhood again and return him to us as wise and capable a leader as you are yourself. Give me this promise, and you may have my daughter as your wife."

He looked at Tadisha, seeing hope and fear mingled in her eyes. Norgu, his ward? To accept the task of teaching him to act responsibly?

But if he refused, he lost Tadisha!

"I . . . cannot guarantee the result," he said finally, "but I will accept the task, Queen Ashuru. I will do my best to turn Norgu into a capable, responsible adult."

Ashuru smiled. Tadisha absolutely glowed. Kamas grinned at him.

Then Ashuru stood, holding out her arms. "Then welcome to our family, son!"

There were hugs all around. Kamas said, "I've always wanted a brother! But by taking Tadisha away, you're certainly giving me a job."

"Want to trade?" he suggested. "You take Norgu, and I'll take the Karili."

Kamas laughed. "No, I think I got the better bargain."

"You're wrong," Wulfston replied, standing now with his arm around Tadisha's waist, "no matter what she costs, Tadisha is the best bargain of all!"

He left Tadisha and her family to make wedding plans, and went to tell Lenardo.

"I wondered how long it would take the two of you to figure out that you were meant for one another," Lenardo told him with a grin. "Congratulations! I needed some good news."

"Why? Is there something wrong that I don't know about?"

"We've hit a block in the reintegration of Z'Nelia and Chulaika. Z'Nelia is hiding something behind a barrier so strong that to break it would be to destroy her mind, and probably Chulaika's as well."

"What can you do?" Wulfston asked.

"I don't know. In my training at Gaeta I Read a patient with a similar block. He had been there for months, in a coma, just like Chulaika. The Healers could not get through it. And while I was still there the man died; his body just wasted away because we could not reunite his mind to it."

"And you didn't have Adepts to strengthen his body. At least Aradia and I were able to keep Nerius alive until you came to help us rid his brain of that tumor we could not Read. Is there any way I can help you with Chulaika, Lenardo?"

"I don't see how," the Master Reader replied. "But it can't hurt your training as a Reader to get more experience, so why don't you join us in the rapport tomorrow?" He laughed. "Your Reader's training is all upside-down, Wulfston! We've never worked on the most basic lessons, and you've plunged right into healing sick minds."

"Well, I'll leave Norgu's mind to you, if you don't mind," Wulfston told him. "But yes, I'd like to Read what you do to try to help Chulaika."

So the next day Wulfston joined Lenardo in the rapport. Ashuru was content to beg off, as she had a royal wedding to plan.

Wulfston didn't know quite what he expected, but it wasn't the calm, peaceful emptiness he found when he followed Lenardo into the mental landscape now inhabited by Chulaika/Z'Nelia. There was no volcano now; no battling figures wrestled to the death. Instead, there was something like a long, empty corridor, featureless, disappearing into nothingness in the distance.

Slowly, Wulfston became aware that the disorientation he felt came from the fact that there were really two corridors occupying the same space, not quite overlapping perfectly. In the physical world, that would make no sense. Here, he understood that the corridors were the twin sisters' lives from past to future, merging together to form one personality that would not be either of them, but a new person formed from all the past experiences of both.

This time he and Lenardo did not take shape; they did
not participate, but merely observed. Their point of view
shifted down endless miles of corridor, so much the same
that they might as well have stayed still, until finally the
two corridors began to separate. Here there were colors
and sounds, then shapes.

//Here the integration ends,// Lenardo told him. //There
is a memory here that Z'Nelia refuses to share, and until
she does, the integration cannot be completed.//

Wulfston "looked" around. It wasn't seeing, though; it
was Reading, that sensing different from his other senses
that he was becoming pleasantly accustomed to. He discovered where the separation began, explored along the
spectrum from integrated new personality through mingled strands of Z'Nelia and Chulaika, to where it was only
Z'Nelia—and within that area a perfectly literal "mental
block"—a mind barrier so solid that it might as well be a
physical wall of steel!

//What in the world could she have to hide behind
that?// he wondered—

And knew the answer!

The block remained. He did not penetrate it.

Yet he *knew*, as plainly as if it were his own memory,
what Z'Nelia was hiding—no, was being *forced* to hide!

The memory was from the time Z'Nelia had almost died,
after she saved Johara by loosing the volcano, and then
was struck down by the Savishnon spy. Her spirit had
wandered the planes of existence between life and death,
perhaps seeking the plane of the dead, unable to find it
because her body was still infused with her indomitable
will to live.

But of those memories only one was blocked, a memory
of terror, of fleeing, lost, from one plane to another until
she encountered—

Pure evil!

A mind even more warped and twisted than her own, a
figure of female depravity, ancient and withered, kept

alive by secret, forbidden methods. A spider hidden deep within the web that spread throughout an empire, carrying her poisons ever outward to maintain her power—until one man discovered her evil, and brought about her destruction.

She refused to die! She escaped the plane of the dead, and waited impatiently. Eventually fate brought her Z'Nelia, her instrument of revenge!

//Blessed gods!///

Lenardo tore himself and Wulfston out of the rapport with such violence that the pain was almost physical.

One moment Wulfston was in Z'Nelia's memory, face to face with the gaunt figure of evil, and the next, senses reeling, he was sitting cross-legged on the floor of Chulaika's tower chamber, gasping for breath as if the exertion had been physical.

//What—? Lenardo, who *was* that?//

But the Master Reader had closed his mind.

"Lenardo! Who was that?!"

Lenardo looked up, his face drained of color. "Portia," he replied.

"Portia? The old Master of Masters? But how could she hide such evil from Master Readers?"

"She didn't hide it from us all," Lenardo reminded him. He shook his head, as if trying to clear it of Portia's mental touch. "Wulfston—"

"You are the man who stopped her,' said Wulfston. "Your kidnapping was her revenge."

"No." Lenardo shook his head. "It was Z'Nelia she controlled, not Chulaika. It's much more complicated than—" His eyes widened in horror. "Aradia! Wulfston, you and I are her first line of protection. Our child!"

"Go pack whatever you need for travel," said Wulfston, getting to his feet. "I'll tell Tadisha and Ashuru. We must leave at once."

"Your wedding," Lenardo reminded him.

"I don't need a wedding, only a marriage. *Move!*"

Lenardo climbed to his feet, staring at the still form of Chulaika on the bed. "Wulfston . . . how did you get through that barrier Portia placed in Z'Nelia's mind, when a Master Reader could not?"

"It wasn't Reading," Wulfston explained. "I just . . . knew, the way I knew Chulaika was somehow connected to me the first time I saw her. Barak says I have the Grioka's talent."

Lenardo nodded. "Thank you. Go on, now. Tell Tadisha. I'll find the *Night Queen* crew."

It took three days of preparation before they could leave. Wulfston and Tadisha were married in the Shangonu temple, with considerable ceremony despite the hurried plans.

The men of the *Night Queen* were eager to go home, but Zanos had not been seen since the destruction of Z'Nelia's body. There were rumors of a flame-haired white man seen in the Warimu lands, and Wulfston theorized that the gladiator was planning a raid on the slave pens at Ketu. All he could do was wish him well in that endeavor, and be glad he did not have to confront him over the murder of Z'Nelia.

"Besides," Lenardo reflected, "I doubt you'll ever convince him he committed murder. He'll always see the act as a just execution."

"Yes," said Wulfston, "but the execution of the wrong person."

The Master Reader stared at him.

"I never could understand how Z'Nelia had either the power or the accuracy to attack our ship from a thousand miles away," Wulfston explained, "but that was what I thought had happened. But after I confronted Chulaika in Norgu's castle, I realized *she* was the one who destroyed the ship, hoping to strip me of my friends and retainers. She drew the power from every Adept on the *Night Queen*—so much power that her storm got out of control. I'm sure she didn't plan on losing me!"

"You were supposed to be her weapon against Z'Nelia," Lenardo agreed.

"But she didn't have as much control as she thought. She was successful enough turning the storm *I* raised against me, that first day of the pursuit." He shook his head. "We assumed it was Sukuru who damaged the *Night Queen*, but he never had that much power."

Lenardo asked, "What about Zanos? What will he do when he finds out it was Chulaika, not Z'Nelia, who was responsible for his wife's death? And that Chulaika may survive?"

Wulfston could only shrug. "That is a concern for the future. Right now, we have more immediate problems."

Norgu was one of the problems. He was as uncoordinated as a two-year-old child now, and could no longer ride a horse. They had to carry his gross bulk in a wagon, and have someone with him to entertain him along the way, or he fussed and screamed like a baby.

Finally everything was ready. The caravan that would take them to the Great River awaited, and messengers had gone ahead to procure passage on a ship for them. Kamas was in the courtyard, but Tadisha and Ashuru were nowhere in sight.

//Wulfston, Lenardo, come to the tower,// Tadisha's mental voice invited.

Lenardo and Wulfston looked at one another, and the Master Reader smiled. "When you have been married a little longer, you will learn that it's not worth resisting such a request. We will be on the road more quickly if we go see what Tadisha has to show us."

Both Tadisha and Ashuru were in the tower room— along with Chaiku, who sat on the bed grasping his mother's hand.

Chulaika no longer lay helpless in a coma. Her eyes were open, and she focused on the two men with a weak smile.

It was not Chulaika alone, though; the integration was

complete, they Read. This was a new person, Z'Nelia and Chulaika as one.

Her eyes—so like Wulfston's mother's eyes—fixed on him. Her lips trembled, but she was still too weak to say anything. But he could Read what she wanted to tell him. //Thank you. I will be well now. No more fighting.//

Even trying to form coherent thoughts was an effort for her. Wulfston knelt beside the bed. "We are happy for you. Rest now, and regain your strength."

//Yes. Take care of my baby. Love . . . //

"That's right," he agreed. "Love your son. Queen Ashuru will help you raise him to be a great king one day."

He looked up at Ashuru as the woman on the bed drifted weakly to sleep. She was right to make him take Norgu away, he realized. Chaiku had to be allowed to grow up without his half brother's threatening presence, and Norgu would be better off far from Africa's temptations until he learned to value cooperation over conquest.

Wulfston rose and took Tadisha's hand. Her green eyes looked into his for a moment. Then she turned to say goodbye to her mother, and to her homeland.

Hand in hand they followed Lenardo down the tower stairs, to join the caravan waiting to take them to their new life together.

END

What happened in the Savage Empire while Wulfston and Lenardo were in Africa? What is the fate of Lenardo and Aradia's unborn child? Look for the next book in the Savage Empire series, *Empress Unborn*.

About the Authors

JEAN LORRAH is the creator of the *Savage Empire* series, in which *Wulfston's Odyssey* is the sixth book. The first five are *Savage Empire, Dragon Lord of the Savage Empire, Captives of the Savage Empire, Flight to the Savage Empire* (with Winston A. Howlett), and *Sorcerers of the Frozen Isles*. Jean is coauthor with Jacqueline Lichtenberg of *First Channel, Channel's Destiny,* and *Zelerod's Doom* in Jacqueline's Sime/Gen series, and has written a solo novel in that universe, *Ambrov Keon.* She is also the author of the professional *Star Trek* novel *The Vulcan Academy Murders,* and coeditor with Lois Wickstrom of *Pandora,* a small-press sf magazine.

Jean has a Ph.D. in Medieval British Literature. She is Professor of English at Murray State University in Kentucky. Her first professional publications were nonfiction; her fiction was published in fanzines for years before her first professional novel saw print in 1980. She maintains a close relationship with sf fandom, appearing at conventions and engaging in as much fannish activity as time will allow. On occasion, she has the opportunity to combine her two loves of teaching and writing by teaching creative writing.

WINSTON A. HOWELTT is coauthor of *Flight to the Savage Empire* as well as *Wulfston's Odyssey.* He has a B.A. in Mass Communication. A former news writer, he is now a free-lance media producer and director. After writing dozens of stories and articles for fanzines, he made his first professional sale in 1978. He and Jean met through science fiction fandom, and occasionally appear on panels together at conventions. An electronic musician, Winston is planning an album of "spirit music" based on the *Savage Empire* series, and is now working on a fantasy series of his own.